By the Author

The Ghost's Host

Wildflower

Visit us at www.boldstrokesbooks.com

WILDFLOWER

by
Cathleen Collins

2023

WILDFLOWER

ISBN 13: 978-1-63679-621-5

THIS TRADE PAPERBACK ORIGINAL IS PUBLISHED BY
BOLD STROKES BOOKS, INC.
P.O. BOX 249
VALLEY FALLS, NY 12185

FIRST EDITION: AUGUST 2023

CREDITS
EDITOR: BARBARA ANN WRIGHT
PRODUCTION DESIGN: STACIA SEAMAN
COVER DESIGN BY TAMMY SEIDICK

Acknowledgments

I want to thank Barbara Ann Wright, first and foremost, for believing in me and pushing me to do the impossible—turn my little story into a whole darn novel. Without her thoughtful commentary, gentle prodding, and unfailing faith in me, *Wildflower* would never have blossomed into the book it was meant to be.

A giant shout-out to cover artist Tammy Seidick for the incredible work you do to make visions into reality. This book cover is magnificent, and it fills me with incredible amounts of joy.

A huge thanks to Bold Strokes Books and all the people there who made this dream come true—I still can't quite believe this is real life. Thank you, once again, for taking a chance on me and giving me the opportunity to dwell among the excellent authors in your ranks!

For my father, who left us too soon, and for Dan, who loved him unconditionally.

And, of course, for Lori, who has put up with me through all this madness for more than two decades (even when I do something dumb like accidentally shave the dog bald, concuss myself during a harebrained project, or wander into a wayward patch of poison ivy). Since we've made it this far, it looks like you're stuck with me!

CHAPTER ONE

The bare wallpaper of the hallway left me feeling smaller than I already did, smaller than my eleven-year-old body had any right to feel. As we marched past the closed doors on either side, my mother smiled down at me, squeezing my hand before we entered the last door. Her lipstick had smeared a tiny bit at the corner of her mouth, and her hair had a few flyaway strands, like golden whiskers sticking out of her ponytail, the only signs of our mad dash to get out of the house. We were late as usual. If there was one thing I could count on in life, it was my mother's refusal to see deadlines as anything more than gentle suggestions.

Unlike the plain beige hallway, the office walls were covered in colorful hand-painted murals. I ran my fingertips along them, reveling in the texture changes within the swirls of thick paint. I might have hated coming to therapy, but the murals made the loudness of life just quiet enough that the constant inward cringing relented. The colors worked better than any medication to calm the chaos in my head.

Dr. Le Van walked out from behind his desk to greet us as we entered. "Lily. Hannah. My favorite duo."

"Hello, Dr. Le Van," my mother replied, glancing up at the clock and smiling sheepishly. "Sorry about the time. You know how things get."

"I do indeed." He turned and winked at me before clearing his throat. "I thought we might try some painting today. Is that okay, Lily?"

I shifted so my back was to him and continued tracing the mesmerizing ridges of paint on the wall. Painting was boring. I never could seem to get the thoughts in my head to spill onto the paper. It was easier to write down the words and imagine the pictures.

"Tell me, Hannah, how have you been this past week?"

"It's been okay, Doc. It's still hard, though." She sniffled as she spoke. I could hear the rustling as Dr. Le Van pushed a tissue box across the table. "Mark wasn't around much the last couple of years with all the deployments. It still feels surreal. I just don't know."

"Is it as hard as it was last year?"

"God, it's been a year already? Feels like only a few weeks."

"It's been eighteen months, Hannah, but I can see the difference. You seem more centered, less like a stiff breeze would blow you right back out the door. Lily, too. She's making good progress on her journals. Have you noticed any changes?"

"Yes. Not so many nightmares for me, I guess. Lily is still, well, *Lily*. Head in the clouds, nose in a book, and always full of surprises. We've been getting out more to the zoo and such. Saw the reptile show at Lake Tobias last week, didn't we, honey?" I turned and lifted my chin in agreement before looking away. "We're going to head down to Texas in a few days and stay with my parents for a while. It will do Lily good to get out of the city, and to be honest, I just need a break from everything."

"It might do you both some good to have a change of scenery. I have a few colleagues in the Dallas-Fort Worth area that I can contact as far as getting Lily into a good program if you're interested."

The scratching sound of his pen on a notepad crept along the skin of my arms, raising goose bumps. It was awful and wonderful, as if the scratching was deep inside my brain like a cricket inside a big empty castle.

My mother's soft voice smothered the last few seconds of the sound. "That'd be great."

"I know we've talked about this ad nauseam, but you should think a little more about putting her back in school. Lily is making great strides with her social development, and having contact with peers her age might help her to open up a little more. How would you feel about that, Lily?"

I looked at the floor, flexing my fingers in time with my breath, listening to the *ka-thunk* of my heart as it hammered away inside me. School. There was nothing good inside those cement walls, just busy halls and endless noise. The thought of going back there, of forcing myself to sit still in an unyielding chair at a desk that screeched across the tile floor with the barest of touches made me sick to my stomach.

"She's doing great with her work, well past her grade level in everything but history."

"Yes, Hannah, and that is wonderful, but she needs to learn how to deal with social situations and settings where you can't be present. I'd like you to set up a few solo sessions if you can. I think Lily would really like Dr. Coates."

I stepped farther down the wall to my favorite part of the mural: a peacock strutting from behind thick drooping fern leaves. I imagined a huge feathered tail behind me, spreading as wide as the doorway, blues and greens shimmering under the fluorescent lights.

"I'll think about it. Maybe once we come back."

"Hannah, I want you to know that I support whatever

decision you make. My job isn't to undermine your parenting or tell you what you're doing wrong. You know what is best for your daughter. Lily is a smart kid. She's just a little locked-up inside. It might help to spend time with family."

"Hmm. Sorry, Doc, but you've never met my family. My mother is, well, abrasive, to say the least. A hard-core Southern bitch, honestly. Not that I have much of a choice. She and my dad are our only living relatives, and they can offer opportunities for Lily that she will never have here in Pennsylvania."

"What sort of opportunities, if you don't mind my asking?"

"They've got boatloads of money, connections, sway. They live on the Gulf Coast with lots of space and clean air. It was paradise when I was a kid."

"You don't often bring up your past. When did it start seeming less like paradise?"

"After I met Mark. My mother hated him. We couldn't get away fast enough. I've only been back a handful of times in the last twelve years, probably not since Mark's first tour in Afghanistan."

"Does she know Mark passed away?"

"Yes, I talked to my father about it right after it happened. He begged me to come home, but I thought I could handle it on my own. It feels like failure to go crawling back there now."

"It isn't failure to seek the support of loved ones. That is what makes you human. We all need a safe place to land when things are difficult."

I wandered over and sat at the table, reaching for the blue paint. I drew a large feathery-looking P on the paper, then outlined it in green. Underneath, I began writing all the bird species I could think of that began with the letter P.

My mother leaned over, whispering a few more names

in my ear. "Plover, pigeon, oh, and don't forget my favorite, pelican."

I nodded and added it to the list, chewing my lip as I concentrated. Pelican was a good one. I imagined being caught in the stretchy pouch of a pelican's mouth, sloshing back and forth as it sailed over the ocean. The rest of our session floated by as I dreamed about spending a lifetime watching the world glide away, leaning over the edge of the pelican's parted bill.

❖

My grandmother, Dawn, had pulled a few strings and managed to get us on a small plane leaving from a private airfield outside of Harrisburg. My mother and I crossed the tarmac against an early summer breeze that had our hair tangling and waving across our faces, leaving us giggling and breathless by the time we made it to our seats. It was my first time flying, the first time I had even seen a plane up close. It was huge. The wings jutted out like stiff arms, gleaming in the bright sunlight. A wide white staircase had been rolled up to the side, and the hair on my arms stood taller with every step. I wanted to turn and look out over the tarmac behind us, but the crew had already waited long enough for us to arrive, and they shooed us inside before I had a chance to peek over my shoulder. The cabin was quiet, only a few travelers making the southern journey to Texas. I wrinkled my nose at the smell of antiseptic cleaner and new carpet.

My mother raised an eyebrow at me and smiled. "I know. Gross, right? How many seconds till the smell goes away?"

"Fifteen," I responded, starting to count under my breath. Magically, the smell seemed to lessen until I could barely detect it. I took a few more sniffs for good measure. "Better."

"Good job, Lily. Won't be more than a few hours before we're smelling salt water and sand, kiddo. Got your beach bag ready?"

"Yup."

"Good deal. Got your bird book?"

"Yup." I held up the tiny, well-worn pocket guide. Its tattered edges felt like velvet against my skin.

"How about britches? Got your britches on?"

I laughed at her silliness. She crossed her blue eyes and stuck out her tongue at me.

"Good. Take a nap, kiddo. We'll be there before you know it."

The Dramamine she had given me earlier had me feeling drowsy enough that even the excitement of being in the sky with my feathered friends could not persuade my eyes to remain open. I yawned and snuggled in under her arm as the engines whined.

❖

"Lily." An urgent voice broke through my dreamless sleep, sending my heart racing as I felt an invisible fist of wind pressing me deep into the plush seat. The world around me tilted oddly, smelling of smoke and fumes. I felt my mother's arms tighten as she screamed, shielding me from the chaos of the cabin. Other voices, including my own, rose with hers as the cacophonous whistling and whooshing grew louder. Then the noise grew farther and farther away until there was nothing but silence.

I dreamed of my mother in fleeting wisps that reminded me of the clouds. Her pale blond hair, laughing blue eyes, and tender smile wavered around me like dust in the wind. I could feel her glossed lips on my cheek as she made a wet kissing

WILDFLOWER

noise to draw out my smile. In my dark inner world, she had always been the brilliant light that kept me from disappearing altogether.

Slowly, I surfaced from my dream into an entirely new reality. My ears rang, and my mouth tasted like pennies. The explosion, the wild spiraling, and the impact felt like I had watched them from a distance, leaving nothing but the imprint of screams echoing through my brain. My mother's arms were no longer around me but hanging limply forward as she took shallow breaths beside me. The flames that had crackled outside the cabin as we plunged from the sky were still sizzling, though they were quickly dying as the wet foliage and soil smothered them.

The nose of the plane was gone, leaving a gaping hole where the front burrowed into the earth, wrapped in tree trunks and briars. We were tipped forward, leaning heavily to the left, branches and leaves obstructing the view from my window. The smells were strange, acrid, and overwhelming, so I pinched my nose and breathed through my mouth the way my mother had taught me, counting to fifteen. It helped but not enough. I sat still, buckled tight, with sore muscles, a few scratches, and sticky wet trails down the side of my face, dripping red onto my pink shirt.

"Mom?" I tried my hardest not to panic when there was no answer. *Keep calm, keep still, and everything will be okay.* "Mom, please wake up. *Please.*" My whispers sounded too loud, too scratchy, too desperate for her to ignore.

Nothing but the soft flutter of breath passed her lips. I could feel myself shutting down, withdrawing into the safe harbor of emptiness. After a while, it became even quieter, just an occasional soft cough from a seat near the back of the small plane. The June afternoon drifted toward darkness, leaving me to cry softly in the dim light until I could stand it no longer.

"Mom, I have to pee. I don't know what to do. Mommy?" She was unnaturally still beside me, pale and silent, nothing my brain was prepared to face. I told myself she was sleeping. This was not forever, just for now. In a few hours, she would reach over and wake me up, telling me we'd arrived in Texas and I had slept through the whole trip.

The low, rumbling voice of the coughing man startled me. "Come on over here, honey. Come unbuckle this seat belt for me, okay?" He wheezed with enormous effort, pressing one hand to his chest as he spoke. The other hand dangled in the aisle way, purple and angry looking.

Terrified, I did not reply, turning my eyes forward and hugging myself tightly to ward off the shivers that threatened to overtake me. He was frightening, bloody-faced and unsmiling, but he looked as scared as I felt. Minutes marched by as I debated what to do about his pained request. What would my mother want me to do? Would she be disappointed that I was unable to perform the simplest task to help someone in need, or would she be proud of me for not talking to a stranger? Finally, I unbuckled myself, climbed across my mother's still lap, picking my way down the dark, messy aisle over suitcases, clothes, and other loose items.

He smelled sour and metallic. I reached out, my hand trembling, and released the clip for him. He sagged forward with the sudden freedom. The movement frightened me even more, and I lunged backward, scrambling to a safer distance. He sighed and leaned his forehead on the seat in front of him.

"Thanks, honey. What's...your name?" His speech was slow and labored, sweat dripping off him in streams. Soot darkened his skin, making him look as though he had just stepped out of a coal mine.

"Lily." I was confused now that he was free, unsure how much to say or even if I should be talking to him at all. Then a pebble of relief began to grow inside me. He could help my mother, and we could leave this creaking airplane and play in the Texas surf, just like we had planned.

"Hi, Lily. That's a…beautiful name. I'm Jack. How old… are you, sweetheart?"

I looked back toward my mother, hoping she would stir. "Eleven."

"Eleven? Nearly…as old as my Jessica. She's soon thirteen." His thin smile lasted only a few seconds before he groaned through gritted teeth. "Lily, I need you…to take hold of my arm." He tipped his head toward the swollen purple limb nearly touching the floor. "And pull it…forward."

I tentatively touched the gross thing, then recoiled. It felt like an uncooked hot dog, clammy and cold. I gagged at the thought of touching it again.

He gave another brief smile and nodded. "It's okay, Lily…if you can't." Pain was etched in the lines of his brow and oozed along the hissing edges of his voice.

I swallowed hard, reaching forward to take his arm into both of my hands, trying to pretend it didn't remind me of a fat, purply earthworm. "Like this?"

"Yes, just…like that. I'm going to move now. You hold tight. I…might make some…noise. Don't you worry."

I took a deep breath and spread my feet apart for balance, awaiting his instructions. When he gave the nod and jerked back, I held his arm with all my strength, and I heard a loud pop. Jack groaned loudly and slumped forward. My heart thundered in my chest as I watched him breathe the same shallow breaths my mother had taken. What had I done? Who would help us now?

❖

He was silent for hours, long enough to frighten me into thinking he wouldn't wake up again. How was I supposed to be brave without someone to tell me what to do? Cold fingers of fear gripped me tightly. I was alone, small, and scared out of my mind, with no one to help me. By the time Jack's eyes cracked open again, I'd peed my pants and curled up on the floor, too scared to go outside.

"Lily? Oh, Lily...I'm sorry. Honey, are...you okay? Say something...please." Tears leaked down his cheeks as he stared at me on my bed of debris at his feet. "Lily?" He placed a hand on my tense back, but for the first time in my life, I did not flinch at being touched.

I caught a glimpse of his once purple hand that now looked almost normal as it drifted to my shoulder, tangling in my hair. His skin was dark against the paleness of it. I felt his compassion, his need for comfort, and I put my hand over his. He began to sob, fat tears splashing onto the rusty stains on his dark pants. His body shook, but his hand never moved from my shoulder. I pressed against his legs, wrapping my arms around them and clinging as though he were the only thing anchoring me to the earth.

"I'm sorry I hurt you," I mumbled into his stiff pant leg. "I'm sorry."

"Nothing to be...sorry about. You did good. My arm... feels much better." His wheezed words were laced with sniffles. "I'm thirsty. Do you think...find me something...to drink?"

I climbed over the debris in the aisle as fast as I could to the water and snacks in the cabinet Jack pointed toward. Grabbing all I could carry, I picked my way back to him. He gulped the water, ignoring the snacks, so I ate them, finally able to feel the sharp ache of my hunger now that I had a companion.

"I need to ask...another favor, Lily." He closed his eyes

as I waited to hear his request, knowing whatever it was, I wouldn't like it. "Can you…check the others?"

I shook my head vigorously, unwilling to leave the safety of his presence and face what would greet me from the other seats. It was too quiet, too still for anything good to await me. I looked up at him, watching the lines on his brow deepen slightly. His visible unhappiness sent a chill down my spine. What if I didn't do as he asked, and he wouldn't help us? I squeezed my eyes shut and stood. My stomach turned as I slowly made my way down the aisle once more, stopping at each of the others briefly. By the time I got to my mother's seat, my chest was heaving with effort. *Sleeping, sleeping, sleeping,* I chanted silently. I could feel myself drifting away from the situation, floating weightlessly at the ceiling of the crumpled plane, observing.

"Lily. We need to…cover them up." Jack pointed at a cupboard with blankets spilling out.

I obeyed mechanically, shutting out the fear and sickness threatening to take over. After picking through the debris in the aisle at Jack's urging, I was too drained to continue. I curled up at his feet again and slept dreamlessly. Hours must have passed.

I stretched and blinked against the soft light glowing through the broken windows.

Jack was holding a flip phone in his good hand, grimacing at it. "Dammit. Still nothing." He dropped the phone on the floor, giving it a disgusted look.

"Nothing what?"

"No signal." He coughed harshly, a fine mist of blood landing on the seat in front of him. "Gotta wait…it out, I guess."

He began asking me questions in his halting wheeze, smiling encouragingly whenever I answered. I told him about my family, our home, the things I loved most in the world. I told him about losing my father and the mural on the wall of my therapist's office, the family of squirrels that broke into our attic every year and made a mess, and about watching old black-and-white horror movies with my mother. He told me about his daughter, Jessica. She was tan and tall, dark-eyed like Jack and smart as a whip like her mother. He told me about her soccer trophies and spelling bee awards, her blue ribbons at horse shows, her love of reading and science. They lived in a big old house in North Carolina with a porch swing and golden retrievers lounging on the vast lawn. Jack fished around in his torn coat. He handed me his wallet and told me to keep it safe so Jessica's pictures wouldn't get lost.

I took out the first one, watching his eyes mist over as he pointed at Jessica kneeling in a soccer jersey. A long dark braid was pulled over her shoulder as she smiled wide for the camera with straight white teeth and deep dimples. He remained quiet for some time after I put the photo away.

"You are going…to have to go outside. Check it out."

"Why?"

"Find help. Scout around."

Fear reared in my chest once more, squeezing me like a boa constrictor. Why did he want me to leave? What if there was something worse right outside? There could be bears or ax murderers or giant volcanos bubbling just past the trees that covered the windows. I shook my head vigorously.

He smiled slightly and took my chin in his hand. "Brave Lily. Be strong. I know…it's scary. No other way."

He told me what to look for in the woods, things we could eat, things to bring back that he could use for medicine maybe. He warned me to be very careful not to injure myself and showed me where the manual was in the first aid kit that was strapped fast to the wall. He told me how to work the emergency exit and what to look for outside. With the bottles of water all but gone, I needed to find water. There was nothing close by but trees, nothing we could hear or smell through the broken windows, and he told me I might have to walk a bit. He gave me his multifunction wristwatch, showing me how to use the tiny compass so I would not get lost in the impenetrable wilderness.

My first journey was short and terrifying. The trees seemed to reach for me, clawing at me as I fought my way out of the plane. Every cracking branch sounded like bears thundering through the forest to eat me. I raced back inside with my heart pounding, covered in sweat. Jack's gentle smile gave me the courage to try again.

I went out several times, each walking farther than the last, then came scurrying back without finding anything worthwhile. After the fifth time, I walked west, according to Jack's compass, coming over a low rise and hearing water gurgle happily to my left. There, cutting a narrow trough through the trees, a trickle of icy water swirled and disappeared over a rock ledge. I filled all the water bottles and stuffed them into the backpack I had found on the plane. Jack was pleased with my discovery, remarking that we were as good as saved. I blushed with pride at his words, content to be useful.

❖

The next day, Jack sent me out again and again in every direction, searching for any signs of food or civilization. Everywhere I looked there were tall, tall trees. I plucked flowers, nuts, fruits, and berries, packing them into my bag to be delivered to Jack, who examined them thoughtfully. He taught me what was safe, what was bad, what could help soothe his pains and dress his cuts. He told me all about his time as an Eagle Scout, camping in national forests with his troop and how they had nothing but a pocketknife and a magnifying glass and could survive for weeks in the woods. He reassured me that someone would be coming to find us, but it might take them a while, and I had to know what to do in the meantime.

I welcomed the distraction from our increasingly dire situation. Every quest Jack thought up gave me a reprieve from the constant sadness that threatened to overwhelm me. I answered his questions, followed his instructions, and learned what he taught, gobbling up the knowledge like a starving person at a buffet. One of the most fascinating things he talked about was how connected the forest was, how the trees shared a language, and the mushrooms talked deep beneath the soil.

"What do you think...they're saying right now?" he asked, gazing at the leaves pressed against the glass. "Hellos and good-byes? Maybe sharing songs?" His voice trailed off as he hummed a few notes of a song I did not know. The longer I thought about the nameless tune, the more haunting it became, following me wherever I went like an echo.

When not traipsing through the woods, I sat next to him, flipping through my worn bird book, pointing out some of my favorites. My heart squeezed painfully whenever the pages fell open to my mother's favorite, the pelican. I built a little story in my mind about how she had gotten up and walked into the forest, starting a game of hide-and-seek while I covered my eyes and counted.

Because he could not stand or do more than point, I became Jack's hands, his legs, and his lifeline. In a short time, I grew to love him, wholly and without condition. He spoke to me with kindness. He tired easily; our conversations were short but packed with importance. Once, he stopped me before I left the plane in a search for mushrooms.

"Lily, wait. Take these." He pointed to the pile of suitcases. We had been filling them with supplies, keeping them close by. "I want you...to start taking these out...and stash them. This cabin is...not going to be safe soon." I knew what he meant. The smell of the other passengers was almost unbearable in the still air of the plane. They were all covered, including my mother, but the blankets were dampening with fluids and smelled unpleasant enough to make my eyes water. Flies congregated in clouds, creeping over the soft cloth like a moving curtain.

"Where?" I felt the panic swell at the thought of leaving the plane. How would anyone find us? My mother had drilled into me that if I was lost, I should stay where I was and not wander off. How could I leave her behind? What if people came, and we weren't there to be found?

"Some...place safe." Jack drifted to sleep, apparently content that I could figure it out on my own.

"Okay," I mumbled. I tugged on the largest suitcase, putting my full weight behind it and grunting with effort, but it would barely budge. Even the smaller cases were surprisingly heavy. I puzzled over how I would carry them through the thick brush. After a few moments, I realized there was no point worrying about carrying anything if I didn't have a place to take them. I had to find somewhere safe first.

I knew Jack would sleep for a while, and I hopped out of the plane, heading into the woods. It was midday, the sun high in the sky, and the forest was buzzing with life. Dragonflies flitted in and out of my peripheral vision, rabbits scurried through the foliage, and birds threw their heads back in song all around me. The thumping of a woodpecker drilling into a tree trunk echoed loudly. A few feet into the dense wood, I turned to look back. I could smell the leaking fuel, but the trees were too thick to see the small plane unless I was standing right next to it. It was swallowed up by nature. The sky was only visible in snippets, blue peeking around deep green leaves and draping branches.

I walked to my little creek, looking both ways along the scar it left between tree roots and brambles. Taking off my shoes, I splashed my feet in the cold water, spying tiny silver minnows darting back and forth in the deeper patches of still water. The drop-off was steep where the water cascaded over the edge, but I leaned out over, watching it slip across jutting rocks and crash to the small pool twenty feet below. I mulled over how to get down to the pool, making a path with my eyes. Without another thought, I crunched through the underbrush and shimmied down the steep grade until I hit level ground.

The pool was much deeper than I'd imagined, the bottom invisible under the midnight-colored water. Around the edges, though, it was warm and comforting. I dug my bare toes into the squishy mud, where there were only a few inches of water, reveling in the temperature and texture. It was the same the whole way around the pool except near the little waterfall. There, the water had eroded the soil and worn the stones smooth. As I got closer, I noticed an opening directly behind the sparkling curtain of water. It was big, a gaping hole in the rock. For a few minutes, I considered what to do. If it was big enough, I could put all the stuff in there, and it would be safe. Jack would definitely approve of such a neat hiding spot. Gathering all the courage I could muster, I stepped through the spray.

Lost behind the water, invisible and undisturbed, was a surprisingly spacious cavern. Huge quantities of light filtered through the mist in a prism of colors, washing over the dirt floor and rocky walls. The floor graded upward slightly and was bone-dry, despite the thin layer of falls a few feet from the entrance. There were ledges and shelves all around, some only a few inches wide, some several feet. The whole cavern was maybe fifteen feet across but stretched on past the light as the ceiling sloped lower and lower. I crawled around in the dirt, happily acknowledging that this was the perfect nook to store our supplies.

When I returned to the plane, Jack was awake. He looked pleased when I told him about my discovery and made me promise that I would take everything there as soon as I could. I nodded and began stuffing my backpack with things from the smallest suitcase. Once the pack was full, I hefted it on my shoulder, satisfied with the weight. Now that the case was partially empty, that too, was easier to drag, even with the backpack.

The rest of that day was spent moving back and forth between the plane and the waterfall. The distance seemed to grow with every trip, my feet heavier, the brambles thicker. On each return, the smell inside the plane grew worse, the air more stagnant and the flies thicker. That alone kept me moving through flagging energy. My arms became useless noodles by the time evening fell, and I felt tears prickling the corners of my eyes. The adventure of finding the cavern behind the falls lost its luster, filling me with anger instead.

Jack, waking on and off, murmured encouraging words that slowly became unintelligible as I stumbled around in exhaustion. Soon, he was merely grumbling, swatting weakly at the flies creeping along every surface and buzzing annoyingly overhead. I ignored his ill-tempered grunts, choosing to pile the remainder of the supplies onto one final blanket to tie for transport. The last trip to the safety of my hidden cave felt like a thousand miles. I fell repeatedly, scraping my knees into a bruised and bloody mess, barely able to right myself and continue.

Why me? Why was no one here to help? This wasn't a job for a kid. It wasn't fair. I clenched my teeth and threw myself down on the rocky ground.

The trees above rustled in the evening breeze, dancing with one another in the growing shadows. Fireflies glowed and blinked amongst the thick tree trunks. The noises of night began to break through my anger. Crickets chirped, owls hooted, thin branches crackled under the feet of unknown critters in the darkness. The forest sang, waking me from my own darkness. Ashamed of my fit of temper, I crawled back into the plane. Jack was asleep when I reached him. I curled up in the chair next to him and fell into a deep, dreamless slumber.

I awoke to a new day dawning overcast and thick with humidity. To my utter relief, there was nothing left to move. The plane was picked clean of anything Jack had pointed out as worth having, and now the hard part would be getting us both safely outside. I waited patiently for him to wake up and tell me what to do next. When his swollen eyes cracked open, I was holding out a bottle of water.

"No. Thank you...Jessica." He pushed it away gently.

I opened my mouth to remind him of my name, then thought otherwise. "Do you want me to bring you some food?"

"Hmm?"

"Food? To eat? Then we can go to the cave."

"No. Not hungry."

I stared at him in concern, for the first time realizing that whatever was wrong with him had gotten much, much worse. His color looked strange, the contours of his face had changed, and he was no longer squirming restlessly against the constant parade of flies.

He smiled sweetly, reaching out to brush my cheek. "Jessie girl, you're...growing so quick. A weed. Gonna...change the world someday."

CHAPTER TWO

It took Jack one more day to die. During that time, he never once called me Lily, and I did not correct him. He talked to me as if I was his daughter, and I sat quietly, holding his hand. Even my eleven-year-old brain knew that he was seeing exactly what he needed to see in his final hours.

It was almost more difficult than losing my mother because Jack had done nothing but fill me with hope and comfort in the few days we had together. He had kept the grief at bay. I strayed no farther than the brush outside the plane, and even then, it was only to go to the bathroom. The quiet trail of his words in the silence was more of a melody than a conversation. There was no sense to be made of the sounds, just a gentle, flowing hum that drifted in and out like the tide.

In the waning daylight, I could hear rain tapping lightly along the metal overhead. For a moment, Jack quieted, turning left and right, listening, hearing something beyond my ears. He smiled wide, moving his head side to side with the rhythm of the rain, then gave my hand a squeeze and sighed. It was the last noise he made, the last movement, the last smile, and the first true vision of peace I had ever seen.

❖

The rain quickly changed to a fine drizzle, then petered out, but it was just a prelude to the fireworks yet to come. An eerie stillness settled over everything, and the hair on the back of my neck stood up. It was barely light outside, shadows growing thick, and I had an irrepressible urge to run. Every nerve in my body jumped like live wires as I ran from the plane. I dove into the trees, running for the waterfall full tilt when lightning split the sky and lit up the whole world. The pressure tossed me bodily into the brambles as the smell of burning wood rushed past like a freight train. I turned over, terror rooting me to the spot. Flaming embers shot into the sky like flares, raining on the forest, igniting even more small fires, chewing through dead timber, and snapping along vines and trunks. Trails of fire raced along the streams of leaking fuel in every direction. Heat radiated in waves, burning my throat with each breath. As I stumbled to my feet, the skies opened, and a deluge of rain tumbled earthward, dousing the flames that reached for me.

Spurred into motion by the snapping of branches overhead, I took off toward the cave, skidding on my already battered knees down the steep slope until I hit the bottom. I felt the smooth rocks of the falls shiver under my feet when I crossed through the growing wall of water. I huddled in my cave, wet and terrified, lonely, missing my mother and Jack. The previous days of hope and distraction were already a distant memory.

The waterfall turned from a trickle to a torrent, trapping me inside as water boiled over the edges of the pond, raging out the other side into the creek that continued down the mountain. It rose higher and higher, swirling menacingly close. The entrance grew slicker as water crept across the dirt. I pressed myself farther and farther into the cave. Angry droplets flung themselves inside, coating everything within three feet of the opening, even the rocky walls.

For two days, the rain fell without respite. I moved from one ledge to another, gingerly picking the debris out of my bloodied knees and sticks from my tangled hair. It felt like a lifetime of darkness. Even if I had wanted to escape, I could see nothing beyond the foaming rapids. I took small comfort in the smell of the blankets from the plane. The once stomach-turning smell of cleaner now reminded me of my last joyous moments with my mother. I slept through huge swaths of time, losing myself to the white noise of the roaring water.

Between naps, I began setting out everything I had taken from the plane onto the rock shelves of my prison. Mostly, it was blankets, a few meager food items collected from the woods, and several bottles for water, first aid supplies, a few life jackets, tarps, and plastic hoses. I had even taken two broken seat backs that had been easy enough to drag. I slept curled up on one of them. I rooted through the suitcases and sorted those things. There were clothes, toothbrushes, a few bottles of some sort of medication, a couple books, notebooks, and various papers. There was a briefcase filled with documents I didn't understand, but it also had pens and paper, a letter opener, and a pair of sunglasses.

My mother's things were the hardest to go through. Her suitcase had makeup and sundresses, an extra pair of sandals, and a swimsuit. Her sundresses and bathing suit still smelled like roses, her favorite perfume. I had similar things in my own, minus the makeup, of course, along with my journal and carved wooden pencil case. We had planned on visiting my grandparents in Texas, staying in their beach house and spending as much time as possible in the ocean before we had to come home to Pennsylvania. I buried my face in the scent and cried.

I grieved over my memories, the two of us packing,

laughing, and teasing one another about sunburns and sand fleas. We fit together like two puzzle pieces. She fed the monster of my curiosity with books and documentaries, and I chased away the sadness that sometimes crept into the lines at the corner of her eyes. I closed my eyes to remember her soft voice whispering to me:

"Kiddo, we've got places to go, you and me. So pull up your britches, and let's get moving!" She winked, snatching me up in the air so I could flap my arms like wings as we flew around the living room.

For another two days, the torrents eased, but it was still too high to pick my way outside. The sound grew quieter and quieter, and sunlight began to break through thinning layer of the falls in wide, brilliant rainbows. I could hear sparrows and whip-poor-wills singing in the trees, calling to me, their warbles pulling me toward the mouth of the cave. Another sound rumbled much closer, the sound of my empty belly growling loudly. No matter how I tried to ignore it, the gnawing hunger demanded my attention.

I had always felt freer in nature, among animals and fresh air. Though I was scared of the dark and the events of the past days, I was not afraid of being alone. Jack had left me with enough knowledge to scrape by until…what? Until someone came for me? The only person I knew who would look for me had died in the plane crash. No one was left. Was this my punishment for being different?

I hunkered down in my private sanctuary, content to bury my grief in the quiet company of stoic stones. When the rains abated and the water sank low enough to venture out, I found myself more afraid than ever. With Jack's watch through the belt loop of my jeans and his wallet in the back pocket of my shorts, I gathered my courage and stepped from the cave into the bright sunshine of a lovely June day.

There were no sounds other than that of the leaves rustling, birds singing, and small animals rushing about on the forest floor. Occasionally, I heard a low *wub wub wub* high above me, sun glinting off the metal body of the helicopter as it passed overhead. Once, I was sure I heard a dog bark far off in the forest, but it sounded strange and muffled, leaving goose bumps to race the length of my arms. Every snapping twig left me on edge. I stayed in sight of my temporary camp, not wanting to wander farther than a few feet into the woods. When I looked up as I sat on the edge of the pool of water, I could only see a patchwork of blue sky through the dense canopy.

There was barely enough food around the pool to make a meal of, and my belly continually growled with hunger. It pushed me hard enough that I began to taste test anything I could reach, though some of the things I ate left me feeling weak and sick to my stomach. One particularly awful bout of sickness led me to stumble a few feet farther into the brush, startling a tree full of birds feasting on newly ripened mulberries. It was a welcome change from the bitter red berries at the edge of the water and the leafy green plants I had been gagging on. The mulberries were sweet and popped like fireworks as I bit down. With a full belly, curiosity finally got the better of me, and I crept back up the ridge to see the plane.

When I stepped out into the clearing of the crash site, I was awed by the sight. No longer was it three quarters of an aircraft but a twisted pile of metal and char. The trees surrounding it were bent and burned and partially uprooted by the force of the blast. There were other, odder things about it, though: footprints in the mud, paw prints, signs of the debris being rifled through. For a moment, I allowed myself to believe the footprints were Jack's, and my heart leapt into my throat. Was he out there right now, looking for me?

Just as I was about to call his name, I thought back to how he could not stand from the seat of the plane. If he couldn't stand then, how could he have gotten out after I did? These couldn't be his footprints. His shoes were smooth and glossy, not covered with deep tread. I debated following the path they took, seized by indecision. Gritting my teeth against my fears, I started down the path. The prints began to fade out a few minutes into my journey until nothing was left but a single paw print under a tangle of briars. I walked a bit in each direction, listening for the sounds of company in the thick wood, but nothing reached my ears save the sound of the woodpecker drumming away for his dinner. The smell of evening was settling, wetting the carpet of dead leaves underfoot, and I could think of nothing more terrifying than being caught in darkness shared with an invisible stranger.

It was a long walk back to my cave that day, a riot of feelings assaulting my senses while I navigated the slope down to the pool. Everything was gone. Everyone. I spent the last hot hour of the day in the water, lost in thoughts that ran all over each other and made no sense.

❖

I knew exactly how much time was passing because of Jack's watch. A small circle on the face of the watch flipped the date every night when the two hands settled on the twelve. A new day, a new week, a new month; they marched forward with perfect regularity. His gift was as much of a burden as it was a pleasure because in the few weeks since the crash, with pants hanging from my thin frame and my hair knotted with brush, I had not been able to forget the time before this, when I was cared for and loved. My mother's birthday came and went, celebrated by no one in my empty kingdom; then a few days later, mine came and went.

I was twelve now, undernourished and fraying around the edges. Every day was layered with new shades of panic. What if that noise wasn't a squirrel? What if there wasn't any food to be found? What if, what if, what if. I distracted myself with my bird book, spending the hours I was not foraging staring into the trees and identifying anything I could find with feathers. From a lone bald eagle to a flock of tittering goldfinch to a wild turkey who flared his coppery tail at me, I began to realize I was no more alone in the woods than I would have been on the street where I lived. There was so much wildlife that I lost count of the critters I saw.

Once, five weeks post-crash, when following a narrow trail through the briars, I stumbled upon a small hairy pig squealing and thrashing with its leg pinched in a metal trap. I backed away, terrified of the noise, the movement, the tang of fear that wafted in the air. I stepped directly into the path of a large brown and white dog. He bared his long, gleaming white teeth, emitting a low growl. I pressed myself into the thorns to escape. The dog watched me, his floppy ears and amber eyes focused intently on me as I tried to disappear into the forest. I walked miles out of my way to avoid that trail on the way back, looking over my shoulder every few feet, expecting the slavering hound to be inches away and aiming for my throat. The idea of being caught in a trap was added to the growing list of things I did not want to experience. The little pig weighed heavily on my mind, but going back was clearly out of the question.

When my long walk left me turned around, I consulted Jack's compass, trying to remember exactly how to interpret the tiny needle pointing north. It took me three hours to find my way back to the creek and even longer to trudge back up the hill to my little waterfall. I let out a small whoop of joy when I rounded the bend and saw familiar surroundings. Collapsing into the nest of clothing I had made a bed from, I dropped into an unforgiving sleep filled with dark terrors.

Three more times that week, I glimpsed flashes of brown and white in my travels but only once close enough to hear the guttural rumble of his contempt. Each time, I retreated, convinced I was being stalked by the snarling beast. When it finally dawned on me that he was not, in fact, chasing me, I only felt a little bit better.

As the sun rose higher and the temperatures climbed, I found myself spending more and more time inside my cave. One day, when the sun was at its highest and the waterfall not much more than a thin sheet, the cave was lit far into its recesses. I caught sight of an anomaly in the deepest part of the chamber that had been hidden in the darkness, a small crevasse in the wall, large enough for me to slip through. I took a deep breath, steadying my mind to enter and hoping not to get stuck. It was only a few feet long, this narrow passage, and high enough that I could not reach the ceiling with my arm straight overhead. The rough, limestone walls clutched at my clothing like sticky fingers, leaving trails of white dust on the pale pink fabric. The floor angled up and up, steeper than I had expected, dark and otherworldly as my body blocked the flow of light from the main cave. When I popped out the other side, it took several minutes for my eyes to adjust.

In the center of the enormous room, there was a circle of smooth river stones, charred on the edges, looking as though the owner had just stepped away for a moment. The light was sparse; I could barely see, and when I walked toward them, I stumbled over the natural dips and cracks in the floor. I fell hard to my knees, crying out with pain when one struck something sharp. I dragged myself back through the crevasse and into the light to inspect my throbbing, bleeding knee. I sat near the water's edge with my little first aid kit, staring in awe at the shard pulled from the wound in my tender skin. It looked like a tooth, a curved, oversized, terrifying tooth. There was a hole in the wider end and the remnants of what looked like a piece of cord. I turned it over and over, reveling in the satiny feel of the cool bone on my palm. The wound itself wasn't terrible, just a small puncture that I doused with peroxide and stretched a Band-Aid over.

The days piled one on top of the other as I learned to venture farther from camp, looking for more things to sustain my growing hunger for both food and knowledge. It was a day in mid-July, hot as blazes, the air alive with the threat of unpleasant weather, when I stumbled upon a ramshackle cabin in a small clearing a few miles from my waterfall. I stepped from the woods into an acre of thick, weedy grass and was greeted with a familiar growl. Frozen, I focused on the tops of the moving seed heads, trying to locate the dog, who was short enough to be hidden in the overgrown field. I felt a cold sweat break out, and my heart raced thunderously. The muscles in my legs twitched with the desire to run, though my mind was adamant that I stay put. There was a gruff shout, almost like a bark, and the growl faded away. Before I could turn to escape, a gnarled, imperfect set of fingers snagged the sleeve of my shirt, jerking me off my feet, and I was dragged toward the cabin.

"Who the fuck are ya, and what are ya doin' on ma land?" The old man had grabbed my upper arm tightly as he continued to drag me. He smelled of burned wood and had black grime embedded thickly under his fingernails. I yanked hard, trying to disentangle myself from his unwashed grip, planting my feet as firmly as I could.

"Let go," I screamed, kicking and fighting as though my life depended upon it.

He merely laughed at my futile attempt. "Go ahead'n scream. Ain't nobody gonna hear ya, less your mammy and pappy are nearby. And they better be quicker'n ol' Biscuit here." He pointed at the dog that followed, snuffling in the grass where my heels overturned the soil.

"Where are you taking me?"

"Out back to the chop. You'll make a good base for ma soup tonight." He cackled as he hauled me up onto the rickety porch and tossed me into an old camp chair. "Watch her, Biscy," he commanded the dog, who stood rigid, his unwavering stare freezing me to the spot. The man disappeared into the cabin for a few minutes, knocking about, then returned with a rusty shotgun, which he pointed in my direction for a second before he propped it up against the side of the house. He pulled a second chair over, facing the direction I had come out of the woods and plopped his weathered frame down.

"Are you really going to put me in your soup?" I asked in a tiny voice, afraid he'd shoot me, or the dog would leap for my throat.

"Does it look like I gotcha all skinned and gutted? Cain't put a whole kid in a pot, now, can we?" He pulled a pipe from his breast pocket and tapped it on the arm of his chair. "You jes sit there and keep yer trap shut till I figure out what's what." He puffed on the pipe for a long time, waiting and watching the woods.

The wait left me terribly frustrated. If he was going to do something awful, he might as well just get it over with. What was the point of sitting here, watching the grass grow? "Nobody's coming," I finally grumbled, no longer caring whether or not I'd made a terrible mistake in admitting I was on my own to a man who'd already threatened to throw me in his soup.

"Liar." He glared at me, pointing a twisted, bony finger into my face.

That single word slapped the fear right out of me. No one had *ever* called me a liar. I wasn't about to let it go, either. All the anger that had been festering deep down, every last insult and upset I had experienced since the crash whooshed up like lava, burning away and remnants of timidity I had left. "Am not," I replied indignantly, ignoring the dog's warning as I crossed my arms and glared back.

"You mean to tell me some'un up an left a baby in these woods and walked off? Nah. You jes tryin' to set a trap for me. Whatcha after? I ain't got nothin' but Biscuit and ma own two hands. Imma wait right here till your kin come traipsing up."

"Fine, but nobody's coming," I said through gritted teeth.

"We'll jes see about that."

We sat on that porch for hours, not another word passing between us. The dog lay at my feet, dozing on and off; the old man snored away in his chair, but I couldn't decide how to escape. I was miserable and tired, desperate to go pee and so hungry, I could barely think straight. Every time I shifted, the dog lifted his head and pinned me to the spot with his eyes. Soon, darkness descended, and the mosquitos swarmed. The old man slapped a few before he seemed awake enough to remember what we were doing outside.

"Nobody's coming," I said once more, figuring the worst he could do was put me in a stew, and that was surely better than being eaten alive by bugs. He squinted at me in confusion, looking me over once more.

"Why not? You didn't jes sprout up from the woods like a will-o'-the-wisp. Where's your kinfolk?"

I shrugged at his questions, convinced it didn't matter what answer I gave. He wasn't going to believe anything. After a few seconds, he reached over and picked up the shotgun, poking me hard in the ribs as he demanded a response.

"Gone." I gestured vaguely toward the woods.

"Gone where? They up and leave ya in da woods 'cause you're an awful brat or what?" I could see the wheels turning in his head as he squinted at me again. He looked off across the field, his eyes glazing a bit as he chewed the mouthpiece of his pipe. "You didn't come from that plane, did ya?" He cocked his head, eyes widening when I nodded. "No foolin'?"

We stared at each other through the cloud of mosquitos.

"I'm hungry." My stomach growled loud enough to startle Biscuit into alertness.

"So what? This look like an all-night diner? Git going, now. I'm done babysittin'. Already took in one damn stray," he groused, pointing at the dog. "Don't need another." He shoved me down the porch steps and stomped into the cabin, slamming the door behind him.

Under the watchful eye of the dog, I trotted through the weeds and mosquitos and into the trees. The unpleasantness of the day clung to me as I followed the game trails and made my way back home, still hungry, still mad, whirling from the meanness of old men who would threaten to eat a kid. Never again would I allow myself to be caught up by a stranger. Never again.

❖

The next morning, I was awakened by the old man's gravelly voice echoing through the woods. "Hey, kid. Kid? Come on out, kid. I got somethin' for ya. *Hey, kid.*" I could hear him shuffling around the pool. "Where's that fuckin' wisp, Biscuit? Cain't be far. Footprints lead right here."

I waited a few more seconds before peeking around the waterfall. His back was to me, a small satchel strung over his shoulder, and the dog was sniffing around the thick stand of trees at the edge of the water. When I was sure neither would see me, I slipped silently from my cave and along the rocks until I was standing directly across the pool from them.

"Go away," I shouted, making both man and beast leap out of fear. Biscuit barked ferociously a few times before the old man reached out to stroke the velvet brown fur of his ear.

"Tricky little wisp, aren't ya?" He shook his head as he scratched his chin and scanned the area with a puzzled look on his face. I picked up a rock and acted as though I was going to throw it at him. "Calm down, kid. I brought ya some grub."

"Go away. I don't want your food." Waves of fear washed over me as they started to pick their way around the pool, stepping through the small stream that headed down the hill from the bottom end. "I said, *go away.*"

They stopped twenty feet away, a toothy grin on the man's grizzled, unshaven face. "Wild un', huh Biscy? Better watch her, she'll take a nip right outta yer hide, boy." He reached behind him and pulled out a brown paper sack that he tossed in my direction. "Cook it till it ain't pink no more."

I made no move to pick it up. He shook his head a second time and looked around.

"Ya got fire, girl?" Now it was my turn to shake my head. "What the hell ya been eatin' all this time? Well, come 'ere. I'll show ya how to get started. Don't be a sissy. Git your ass o'er here so ya can learn somethin' fer once." He squatted, his old bones cracking and popping as he set about sweeping clean a small area. He arranged stones in a circle like the one I had seen in the big cave, then piled dry, fluffy moss underneath some bigger twigs. He pulled two stones from his pocket and set about clacking them off one another until a spark jumped from the stones to the fluff, sending a spiral of light smoke up into the air. A lick of flame crept up from nowhere, devouring the dry stuff, then caught and held on to the kindling. He was silent while I watched, then raised his eyebrows and tossed the stones over. I tried to mimic his motions, clearing a small area nearby.

"Bigger. Cain't cook nothin' o'er somethin' that little."

I widened my clearing, then searched for stones as he had, selecting ones almost too big to carry. When I had built up a nice circle that garnered an approving nod, I gathered some moss and tinder to place in the center.

"Too green. Git that stuff o'er there," He pointed at a brown patch of moss on a downed log. "And those sticks there."

I followed his directions, checking out the moss and twigs carefully before bringing them back. He pantomimed smacking the two stones together, then pointed at the circle. Try as I might, no matter how hard I hit them off one another, I could not produce a spark. I must have tried fifty times or more, bashing my knuckles repeatedly and snarling at my own incompetence. He made it look so easy. What was I doing wrong? I was so engrossed in my efforts than I didn't realize he had moved up beside me until I felt his hands cover mine. He showed me the correct angle and force to apply, turning my wrists and placing my fingers into safe spots on the stone so I didn't hit them again. Together, we created a few sparks that he let poof out of existence, making sure I knew that he was not going to start my fire for me.

It took almost an hour, and my arms ached with the abuse of cracking the stones. Finally, *finally*, a strong spark flew from my hands into the tinder and caught quickly with a few breaths blown on the embers. Never had I felt such accomplishment. My grin was too big to contain, and the old man barked a laugh as I danced around my little pile of fire.

"Good job, kid. Ya got a name?"

"Lily."

"Figures ya'd have one of those goddamned hippie names. Well, Lil, you go o'er there and git a few long sticks, see? We gotta cook that meat, and we need somethin' to hold it o'er the fire."

We cooked and ate whatever was in the package. It was sweet, tangy, and chokingly gamey, but I was hungrier than I could ever remember being in my life, and I devoured whatever was handed my way. After the food was gone, the man stood and walked off into the woods with his dog, out of sight before I could even question his motives. He left me the two fire stones and a small knife that fit into my hand as though it was made for me.

❖

A few days later, he was once again hollering outside my humble abode. I repeated my tactic of last time, not wanting him to see where I came from to prevent him from following me. They seemed ready when I appeared, neither of them exhibiting the least bit of surprise when I said hello. He held up two rabbits by their back legs and crooked his finger to invite me over. I approached hesitantly, guessing what he was planning on teaching me that overcast summer morning.

I watched in horror as he gutted and skinned the first rabbit, but he pointed to my knife and handed me the second. I tried to hand it back to him. "Uh, no, thank you."

"Kid, you wanna eat, you best learn how."

"I'm not doing that. It's gross and mean."

"Nah. Thing's dead already. Don't feel nothin'. You wanna starve?"

I looked at the pile of guts next to him, then the rabbit I held gingerly between two fingers. "Yeah. I'll starve." I made to put down the carcass, but the look in his eye stopped me cold.

"Then take your sorry ass off this mountain. Go find some sissy town to squat in, 'cause you cain't stay up here and not get your hands dirty." He scoffed. "How come you ain't got people lookin' for ya, anyway?"

"I don't have anyone left."

"Your mammy? Pappy?"

I thrust my chin out, wanting to shock him into leaving me be. "Dead."

"Don't you wanna get back to where you came from?"

"Why? Nobody is there. I'm weird. Nobody likes me."

"Kid, we're all weird. Who cares if nobody likes ya? Fuck 'em." I stared at him in shock, hearing the curse word that I knew was the worst one of them all. "What?" He rubbed the blade of his knife in the grass, cleaning off the blood while I rolled the word around in my brain, testing the idea that bad words weren't really bad at all.

Nothing had happened to him when he'd said it, no strike of lightning or policemen running from the forest to take him to jail. I wondered briefly if he would yell at me for saying it out loud, but I couldn't bring myself to try. Instead, I just breathed out my mouth and let my lips form the word without sound. I felt naughty and grown-up all at the same time.

He stuck his blade in the dirt and looked me straight in the eye. "Nobody else to come for ya, huh? Well, I guess we got a lot in common then. But that don't excuse you from learnin' the basics of survivin' out here. Now *cut*."

I glared at him, angry that he didn't seem to care that I was all alone, and angrier still that he wanted me to butcher the rabbit. He was right, though, not to dwell on the loneliness. If I could do for myself, he could go back to his cabin, and I could figure out what to do next. I sighed and reached for my knife.

It was gross and terrible, taking an animal apart like that, but I would never have given him the satisfaction of seeing me fail. I gagged repeatedly, turning away when my fingers touched the wetness within. It was not pretty, the ragged cuts and gore, and he made sure to point out every mistake. When both rabbits were sufficiently butchered, he showed me how to roast them over the fire, and we ate in silence.

After that, he showed me how to make pine needle tea with boiling water. "Good for what ails ya," he said, pulling a jar out of his satchel. "Honey. Sweeten it right up. Drink this stuff every day, and it'll keep your teeth from fallin' out."

We went on like this for almost a month, well into the blistering heat of August. He would arrive as soon as the sun rose and call me out. I learned to set wire and metal traps, process the small game I caught, and cook it with, if not skill, at least efficiency. He was a man of few words and a vast knowledge of the mountains, so I did my best to put aside my anger and listen. Our time together was filled with unanswered questions. One particularly hot morning, as the temperature soared at daybreak, he sat with his dirty feet in the water and spoke.

"Kid, ya got spirit, that is for sure. Jes remember, there ain't nothin' you cain't do. When I was a boy, my pappy whipped ma hide raw 'cause I was too sissy to turn out a pig. Sent me out in the woods with his shotgun jammed into ma back, ah, near seventy some years ago an told me I better git out till I could come back a man. Took a week for me to catch ma first critter and spit it. My ol' man didn't let me in the house till he seen me do it, too. Next day, he got hisself ate up by a mountain lion. My mammy didn't take that so good, an she run off to who knows where, left me and my kid brother all alone. He died of fever after a snake got 'im. Then it was jes me. Ne'er bothered me none, being solo, fendin' for myself, didn't want no responsibilities. I seen hikers an hunters crawling along like they got business up here in ma woods, leavin' trash all o'er, but I ain't never seen no kids runnin' round. This place..." His crooked hands swept around him in a wide circle, gesturing to the sanctuary of his mountainside. "This place ain't for them. This is ours. Yours and mine, lil' wisp. We're the keepers of this piece of heaven, right here."

We sat quiet for a long time after that, both lost in our respective thoughts. He chewed the end of his pipe, and I, well, I was caught up in the joyous knowledge that he thought I belonged. I hadn't considered that I would be here forever, and he seemingly hadn't considered that I wouldn't. He coughed, deep and wet, into the hanky in his back pocket, then rose and walked off, Biscuit trailing his heels. There had been no other lesson, just his roundabout admission that he wanted me to stay, that he was offering this world to me. It was a strange gift, for sure, but it felt like one I had been waiting for my whole life.

It was terribly different from civilization in those woods. They were old and overgrown, life-giving and dangerous. The smells were fresh, earthy, and rich, the sounds, a symphony. Nature fed my curiosity with flora and fauna. I did not have to pretend I was a part of this delicate ecosystem as I did back home in Pennsylvania. The longer my feet explored the wild in which I resided, the more I longed to melt into it. Every day that passed saw me growing taller, more confident, fearless. There were missteps. I walked through a poison ivy patch before the old man could point out the plant. I bloodied my nose and almost lost a finger setting a trap. Each time, I heard the *tsk* of my companion and endured his short, gruff lectures and doctoring as stoically as I could manage.

I began to get careless in my actions, forgetting some of the hazards of my home. After a night of endless drizzle, I careened out from behind the waterfall, minding only the fullness of my bladder and not the slick rocks below my feet. Three steps onto the rocks, my bare feet whipped out from under me on the algae-coated surface. In slow motion, I flailed my arms, almost righting myself before toppling forward. The rocks rushed up to greet me with such force that the whole world turned black. When I opened my eyes, I met the concerned stare of the old man as he knelt over me.

"Kid, you is dumber than a box a rocks," he yelled, putting a hand to his chest as he thumped backward on his butt. His clothes were soaked, and Biscuit was shaking water out of his fur all over us. "What the hell you thinkin'?"

I blinked up at him with confusion. Everything hurt, even breathing. My mouth tasted like cotton-covered pennies, and I was half-naked. The remains of my last decent shirt lay next to me in the grass, covered with blood and torn in half. I licked my lips and felt the sharp edge of a chipped front tooth.

"What happened?"

"Damned if I know, but you was floatin' like a log in the middle of the water. Bashed up your face and shoulder. Biscy helped drag you out like a big ol' catfish. I had to rip up that rag you been wearing to stop the bleedin'."

"I fell."

"No shit, kid. Damn near kilt yourself, too. How many times I gotta say this ain't no place for foolin' around?"

"S...sorry." I hiccupped, trying to hold back my tears, but with my pounding head and aching body, I couldn't stop the tide.

"Aw, knock it off, kid. You'll be fine. Ain't nothin' that won't heal. Well, 'cept that tooth, but not much I can do about that."

He was right, of course. I healed fine with nothing but a jagged scar on the top of my shoulder to remind me of my carelessness. The old man sat with me for three days to make sure I was all right, tending my wounds with honey and mashing up food so I could chew with my sore mouth. He kept the fire burning, covering me with his own shirt and braved the mosquitos bare chested. When I was finally back on my feet, he brushed it off as though nothing had happened, trekking back to his cabin, leaning heavily on the walking stick he always carried.

I had broken Jack's watch in the fall, cracked the face, and it had filled with water. The compass part still worked, but the little arms indicating the time and date no longer moved. I felt ashamed that my stupidity had ruined something so important. My tears did not fix the cracks, so I dried it off and strapped the watch around my arm. The bird book that had been in my pocket fared even worse. The pages glued together, and the ink bled. It was a lesson I would not soon forget.

Biscuit and I formed a wary bond, neither trusting nor affectionate, just a general acceptance of each other's presence. He did not welcome me onto the old man's property, and I never went there on my own. Our relationship lived and breathed at the waterfall. Soon, both became aware of my cave, though they didn't make any attempts to follow me inside.

With fire, I was almost self-sufficient. I could keep away the nocturnal predators, the bugs that swarmed at dusk, and my own suppressed fears. I learned to make a torch, and with that, the cave was truly mine to explore. The first time I took fire through the crevasse and into the huge chamber beyond, I was mesmerized. Not only had someone lived here before me, but they had made murals of red and black high up the limestone walls. Handprints, stick figures, and animals of all sorts paraded across the glossy surface. I spent hours looking at them. The circle of stones was one of four that spread out on the dirt floor. There were other, smaller caverns, mostly just deep recesses in the rock walls, and in them, I found rotten baskets that fell to bits when I touched them and dusty but still useful pottery covered in spider-cracked glazes. The long, curved tooth I had pulled from my knee after my first journey was one of a set that lay near the first stone circle. The old man said they were bear teeth, a collection of sharp canines pulled after the hunt and drilled at one end to hang from a necklace. He even gave me a cord and threaded it, spacing the teeth with small rabbit vertebrae so I could wear them myself.

The old man's visits became less frequent as the fall approached, his cough worse, and the eighty-some years of his existence showed more and more in the haggard lines of his sagging flesh. In mid-November, as the crisp air nipped at my exposed skin, and the leaves crunched underfoot, Biscuit was the only one to appear. I made the hike to his cabin with the dog glued to my side. One entire wall had finally collapsed, leaving the inside of the cabin completely exposed, and wildlife had already begun scavenging in the bare cupboards. I had never been inside, not because I wasn't allowed but because there was nothing in there he had to share, just a cot, a few pots and pans, and the barest of necessities. It seemed as though the things I had rescued from the plane were luxury items compared to the furnishings of the dilapidated cabin. The only things he had of value were tucked neatly in the satchel he always carried: his tin mug, his fire stones and knives, a length of coarse rope, a few rusty fishhooks, a magnifying glass, and his last two jars of honey.

I called out a hello and knocked on the flimsy door, but

there was no answer. It felt wrong to walk into the cabin, like I was an uninvited guest. Biscuit, not waiting for me to enter, just ran to the side that had fallen and climbed over the debris. Inside, I found the old man cold and stiff on the little cot, as though he had fallen asleep, and time had stopped. His walking stick was propped by the door. It didn't seem the same as the frightening death that my mother experienced but more like Jack's quiet last moments. He looked peaceful, relaxed, like he belonged to this time and place.

For the briefest of moments, I was lost, adrift on a sea of loneliness and misery. This gruff old man had given me the last few months of his life, caring for me in his own way, teaching me how to live on his mountain. He'd trusted me with this incredible paradise despite my shortcomings. Could I survive without him? Was there any point in trying?

Biscuit whined, pawing at the grayish hand that dangled off the side of the cot, then turned to me with pleading eyes. I covered him completely with the blanket, picked up the satchel, two traps hanging on the wall, and the walking stick, then headed for the door that I could barely see through my tears. The dog and I made our way back to my cave in silence, grieving a man whose name I never knew.

CHAPTER THREE

We wintered well, Biscuit and I, in the larger chamber that kept us warm and dry. The stone circles lined up with some crevasse in the cathedral-like ceiling beyond my vision, whisking the smoke from the cave easily. There was enough small game to keep our bellies full and our spirits up. There was snow in the mountains, though not nearly what I was used to up north. It was fine, powdery, and short-lived.

The ice was more dangerous, sneaking up, freezing the edges of my pool, and making the distance to the cave treacherous. I slipped once and fell into the freezing water, slicing open my hands on razor-sharp shards as I clawed my way out.

Biscuit was far more agile than I ever hoped to be, but he never strayed more than a foot away whenever we entered or exited the cave after I had fallen in. When the deepest cold set in, we snuggled beside the fire, my fingers buried in his soft coat, his nose tucked under my arm. Our friendship, once tentative and conditional, morphed into mutual respect. He became my guardian, my partner, and my champion.

I pulled out the few books I'd scavenged from the plane and spent hours scouring them. My reading skills had been advanced ever since I could remember, but I was rusty after so long without using them. There was a romance novel, a thriller, and several thick, incomprehensible manuals that left my eyes crossing as I tried to decipher the diagrams and descriptions. I plunged through the manuals by firelight, eventually giving up, tossing them back into one of the suitcases and tucking them up on a ledge. The books I read out loud to Biscuit, who stared intently and listened as I stumbled over long words and strange sentences. The romance novel made me blush uncomfortably at times, so I read those scenes silently, not wanting to say the words aloud. I also began to write in my journal here and there, events of the day or new birds I had seen, using my knife to sharpen the pencils.

We had run-ins with a few unfriendly forest dwellers as we fought over the same resources. Biscuit met the business end of a porcupine, which ended with hours of yelping as I picked spine after spine out of his velvety muzzle, and I came face-to-face with a young mountain lion cleaning his paws after feasting on my trapped pig. Lucky for me, while we were both incredibly stupid, he was young enough to feel threatened by a skinny child screaming and waving a stick. He ran off without doing me any harm.

I made a little altar in the outer cave on a ledge nearly two feet wide and ten long, on which I placed Jack's wallet and Jessica's picture, my mother's makeup case, the old man's gnarled wooden walking stick, the ruined bird book, and my pair of outgrown shoes. These were things I would look at daily, reminders that I had people to miss. The grief I felt had hardened to a little stone in the pit of my stomach, but it never really left. It was pointless to cry, just a waste of energy and time, so instead, I used the shreds of my sadness to fortify me against the cold. I left markings on trees, sometimes names or pictures, but mostly, I carved out a circle and added the dots to represent those I had loved.

I ran barefoot through the forest, pretending I was a fairy, developing thick callouses on the bottoms of my feet. The bitter weather ebbed and flowed, storms crashed, trees budded. Spring was clawing its way out of hibernation, wreathing the Ozarks in a flurry of growth, and with it came a burgeoning of new life.

The first mother I encountered left both me and Biscuit shaking with fear as we raced through the brush back to our sanctuary. The black bear, protecting her pair of boisterous cubs, must have spotted us long before we knew she was there and careened through the forest to chase us away from her vulnerable offspring.

We were panting with exertion when we reached the pool, feet and paws slapping through the cold water, leaping through the falls to the mouth of the cave. The fear retreated once we were inside, and I laughed, patting the soggy dog to soothe his disheveled temper. The bear, having long since given up the chase, was probably miles away, enjoying the beautiful weather with her youngsters.

Occasionally, we caught glimpses of tawny fur through the foliage, just a hint of the predator that lurked in the hidden passages of our playground. We steered clear of any trail that showed one of his huge prints, whether that meant walking a mile out of our way or giving up prime rabbit territory. I knew he was the king, and Biscuit and I, well, we were just lowly trespassers in his kingdom. I learned to walk through the forest like a shadow and read the smell in the air for weather changes. I became as in tune with the environment as that big cat, and as nervous as he, too. Any strange smell or sound sent me scurrying back to safety. Despite feeling brave with a dog at my side, I knew I was just a girl with a pocketknife and two stones, nothing that could save me from becoming something else's breakfast.

Biscuit did his part to protect me, alerting me when an animal approached, herding me away with raised hackles and bared teeth. As we hunted young pigs on an early summer day, we stumbled into the path of a boar, rank and angry, with a thick hide of bristles and sharp tusks turned toward me. He was double my size at least, and his yellow eyes flashed with murder. He charged before we even recognized the situation, and Biscuit took the brunt of the hit. We both flew, landing in brambles, then scrambled away with the boar in hot pursuit. Unlike the mother bear, this creature would not be dissuaded. He cut down weeds and saplings alike, gaining ground with every step. I raised my arms to fend off branches that slapped across my cheeks like whips and wrenched the hair from my head in clumps. I felt the hot breath of the boar on the back of my churning legs, and I began to realize I could not outrun him. Just as I thought I would collapse, we burst through a line of trees into a clearing, startling a pair of men who were climbing out of their tent. Their presence distracted the boar long enough for us to disappear back into the woods, shouts echoing in our wake. The sound of a single gunshot pierced the air.

I followed Biscuit in a wide arc around to the trails that would lead us back to the cave, slowing to a tired walk. People. There were people on the mountain. They were the first I had seen since the old man. As we arrived at the waterfall, I dropped onto a fallen log, lying the length of it and staring through the leaves overhead. It was a shock, for sure, to be reminded that I wasn't the only person left on the planet, that an entire world still existed beyond the wilderness.

Indecision gnawed at me. Should I go back and find them, or should I stay where I was? What if they were bad people? I thought again of the old man and his initial threats to toss me in the soup pot. He was hard and demanding but far from the devil I'd thought he was at our first meeting. Maybe they would be the same. Maybe I could find safety with them. Would I be happy to go with them, back to…what?

It wasn't just distance that I felt from my old life. I felt removed, as if crash-landing on this mountain had been my fate all along. As if every bee, every bird, every flower had been waiting for me to fall out of the sky and into their world. I was Lily in Wonderland. My home was safe, warm, and comforting, and even a little bit magical. I understood the old man and his need to remain free in the mountains.

Sighing, I decided to wait until morning to visit the clearing again. A good night's sleep and a fresh day would be my guide. I would watch the people, then make up my mind. Biscuit and I retreated to the quiet cave, lulled to sleep by the steady whooshing of water over the falls.

❖

Morning dawned with heavy fog that hung low and danced around the tree trunks, making for a treacherous journey along the route we had run the day before. Biscuit, tenser than usual, walked a few steps ahead of me, tail straight in the air, and the fur along his back lifting with every sound around us. Old wet leaves squished underfoot, and the remnants of sweet-smelling tree blossoms, thumb-sized and browning, stuck to my ankles. I grazed along the way, sampling newly ripe raspberries and blackberries. The thorny branches left welts on my forearms, but the fruit was tart, and the joy of picking it fresh was worth the scratches.

It wasn't a terribly long walk, following meandering game trails through the wet morning, but we did not hurry. The farther we walked, the more I could sense a change. The birds were oddly quiet. The happy chaos of wildlife chattering was absent, and as we got closer to the clearing, the hair on my arms stood up. I looked around, worried that the boar would soon be on our heels again, but the brush around us was still. Biscuit lowered into a slink, his ears flattening, tail low to the ground.

I put one hand on his back when we reached the clearing, stopping him from walking out. The smell was awful, like blood and death hanging in the still air. The fog had lifted a bit, revealing an empty spot on the trampled grass where a tent had once stood. In its place were piles and piles of guts. The boar was off to the left, shot through the neck. As we stepped out, I could not believe the vastness of the destruction. Deer parts, turkey feathers, and tufts of fur littered the clearing. None of this had been here the day before, just a tent and two men. Two men I had almost convinced myself to trust. Two men who'd left a graveyard in their wake.

It wasn't just the animals left on the spring grass but garbage as well. Wrappers, plastic shell casings, cigarette butts, and half-crushed beer cans were everywhere. The fear drained out of me, and in its place grew anger. How dared they leave a beautiful place like this in such a state? What kind of people came to the woods and did this sort of thing? What would they have done to me if they'd found me? I shivered at the thought.

❖

Try as I might, I could not preserve food. I found that no matter what I attempted, the meat spoiled, the fruit rotted, and the smell drew in unsavory characters like bugs and skunks. I lived day by day, blowing through time like dandelion fluff on a brisk breeze. My clothes were worn to tatters, and those that weren't no longer fit. I was gaining length but not width on my diet. My hair grew thicker, uncontrollable, twisting in knots that I could never quite untangle. I suffered scrapes and scratches, lumps and bumps, random bouts of diarrhea and vomiting from eating things I shouldn't have.

That spring and into the summer was a time of discovery, achievement, and abandon. Biscuit and I explored miles upon miles of terrain up and down the mountainside. We never returned to the old man's collapsing cabin, never to the clearing where the two men had left their garbage, and never beyond the wide river that my little stream coursed into, where the land grew flatter, the earth marshy, and alligators hid just below the surface. I climbed trees that felt like skyscrapers, scaled rock walls that seemed to tower overhead, and washed myself in the crystal-clear springs sprinkled throughout the landscape. Some days, after my skin turned a golden brown in the constant sun, the only thing I wore was the bear tooth necklace rattling against my prominent collarbone and occasionally, Jack's watch around my bicep.

The compass still worked despite the abuse it had received from my childish exuberance. I no longer needed to use it, instead following the path of the sun, the shadows, and natural landmarks, large and small. I came across curiosities in my travels as well. Sometimes, it was a strange skull, picked clean and bleached with age, sometimes a piece of litter from an inconsiderate hiker, and once, a crudely carved, moss-covered stone statue buried deep in the saturated soil near the river. I collected clay and ash in my cracked pottery, adding my own drawings to the ones that danced overhead in my cave. At times, I painted my own skin and played make-believe games with the long-suffering dog, who also endured my artistic abuse. He would puff out an aggravated sigh but was too gregarious toward me to offer any resistance.

I reached the summer of my thirteenth year, having spent a

full year in the Ozarks. My toughened feet skimmed as lightly over the forest floor as the white-tailed deer, who melted away into the trees like ghosts when I happened upon them. My shoes had long since been outgrown and worn through. When the weather was bad or the bugs too tenacious to ignore, I wore shirts scavenged from the suitcases, and they dangled low and wide, so I began tying them tight around my waist with a string I had pulled from a pair of sweatpants. I could not bear the thought of pulling out my mother's sundresses. The inside of the suitcase still smelled faintly of her perfume, and every now and then, I would crack it open and breathe it in until the pain was too big to handle.

Occasionally, I would stumble upon a gun-toting stranger high up in the woods, and I would watch from afar, content to be the invisible observer. Once or twice, as if feeling like they were being watched, they would shade their eyes and scan the trees, never locking eyes with me. I would follow them like a shadow for hours on end, my stomach roiling at the memory of the clearing filled with death.

It was one of these men who nearly picked me out of the voluptuous pine I crouched in while watching them cook over a campfire. The three men had been quiet in their tents all morning, finally stirring as the sun was highest in the sky and baking the dampness from the forest floor. They stretched and scratched, making gruff conversation over a newly lit fire and a red cooler. The sun inched across the sky while I sat immobile on a thick branch. Biscuit, probably bored with our hours of observing, took off in pursuit of some small critter, drawing the attention of the men who had been guzzling and crunching cans of beer during their meal.

All of them grabbed their rifles and aimed into the woods, one firing two shots into the trunk inches from my head, shouting to his companions that he was shooting at a mountain lion. They shouted to one another for a few moments before starting in my direction. I didn't wait to greet them, landing quiet as a fly on the dry needle bed and bolting off in the direction Biscuit had taken. I could hear them yelling through the trees behind me:

"Heard something over here."

"They'll pay big for a cougar."

"Not if we don't shoot the fuckin' thing, Tom. Where'd it go?"

"Jeezus, boys. If you don't shut your damn traps, we'll scare *everything* off the whole damn mountain."

I eased my way through the underbrush, not disturbing a single branch. Their voices inched closer to me, sending my heart thundering with panic. I closed my eyes, hoping Biscuit had gotten far enough away that the men would not find him. Booted feet crashed through the leaf litter near my hiding place.

"You bring the thermals?"

"Shit. I left 'em in the tent. Well, I'm *sorry*. It's not like I expected to be out hunting in the daylight."

"Bah, I think we lost it anyway."

"It'll be back. We'll bait the station with the leftovers and wait another night. Won't be too hard to pick it off while it's distracted by some good grub."

"Yeah, I guess."

The footsteps and voices faded back the way they had come, but I waited for what felt like an eternity before I crept out from the safety of the brush. Fear evolved into anger as I walked back to the cave. These men would kill whatever they fell upon. There had to be a way to send them back to wherever they came from and save the mountain from their poisonous touch. Biscuit padded up to me as I walked, turning toward home as though he had never left my side.

No matter how long and hard I thought, I could find no solution to the problem. Clearly, they did their hunting at night, and I would not be safe from them in the darkness if even the wary wildlife couldn't escape them. If only I had the old man to tell me what to do. Or Jack. Or my mother. A bitterness filled me as I thought of everyone I used to have. Maybe it was safer for me to be alone so I could not lose anyone else. I was better off alone.

❖

The sun rose and fell, the moon waxed and waned, the rhythm of nature drummed on and on, and I followed obediently. I kept up with my journal, filling it with memories and daily life, questions I could not answer, and leaving whatever sadness I felt scrawled along the pale paper. It was barely legible and poorly written, only a few sentences a day or sometimes none at all, but it kept me tethered to my mother, who loved all the words I wrote. I could almost hear her soft voice encouraging me every time I picked up a pencil.

It allowed me to keep track of time, though not the dates themselves as days slipped past quickly in the mountains. The seasons were easy: warm, hot, cool, cold. I could tell the changes by the smells in the air and the leaves overhead. The weather brought new challenges, and even something as simple as rain added an element of danger to everyday tasks. Trees in wet soil were flung to the ground when the wind kicked up, obscuring game trails and leaving travel even more difficult. The rotting logs brought mushrooms but also hid other hazards like venomous snakes whose fangs terrified me more than any other animal in the woods. The first and only time I had stumbled upon an angry snake, it lashed out, striking a tree right next to where I stood and startling me into a panicked flight down the trail.

My second autumn rumbled through with incredibly severe thunderstorms, hail, and dark ugly clouds. The nights grew chilly with dampness, and the soil sucked at my feet, deep and boggy. It was a lean time, my traps hanging empty or the animal torn free by predators, and the wild forage rotted before I could salvage much. Both Biscuit and I were ribby and pathetic as winter approached, me racked with coughs and low-grade fevers. Ironically, it was the first snow that saved us from starvation, freezing the top layer of sod and leaving game trails clearly visible once more. I set the one remaining heavy trap I had, with its snapping jaws gaping open under a thin coating of fluffy white snow.

I checked it the next morning, shuffling along in exhaustion, expecting nothing. The trap itself was snapped shut with nothing in its teeth, but a thick trail of blood led me off the path and into the heavy underbrush. There, covered in snow and debris, was the half-eaten carcass of a small deer that had been torn from the trap by something large and toothy. The bones had been gnawed and broken, insides spilled, and most of the good meat taken, and I was terrified that the killer was still close by. My terror was tempered, however, by the knowledge that this was enough for us to share, and I could not pass up the opportunity. I carved off large chunks, ignoring the headache that bloomed with my efforts. When I had finished, I skewered the meat with a stick and carried it home draped across my weak shoulders. Biscuit and I ate like royalty that day and the next three, the meat keeping well in the freezing air.

It marked a turning point, a new dawn, as the sickness and weariness drained away with nourishment. I began to follow the big cat tracks instead of avoiding them, learning where he stashed his kills and risking my neck stealing enough to keep our bellies full. I never knew whether he was nearby, watching, stalking, and I did not care. When I caught something bigger than I could eat in my trap, I took my share and dragged the rest into the woods as a gift to the cat. I called him Henry.

Time began to mean less and less to me as it trickled by. I was ruled only by the weather and my own limitations. Toward the end of my third year in the mountains, Biscuit slowed down, grunting with effort when he had to rise and groaning long and low when his old bones settled for a nap. I worried about him day and night, bringing food and water into the cave for him when he was too tired to leave. One day in the earliest blooming of spring, he moseyed out of the cave and sunned himself along the bank of the pond, a content look upon his face. He did not want to go back in the cave, so I slept outside with him two nights in a row. The weather was chilly but fair, and his thick fur kept both of us warm under the blanket.

The third night came and went, and when I opened my eyes at the break of day, I was alone under the blanket. I called and called, searching everywhere I could think of all day long, and short of one barely visible paw print down a well-used game trail, I could find no signs of my best friend.

Hours passed, then days, and Biscuit did not return. My frantic scrambling through the thick wilderness left me covered in scrapes and bruises, yet, I kept going. Beyond food, my only thoughts were of Biscuit. I blamed the men who hunted on the mountain. I blamed Henry the mountain lion. I blamed myself for not keeping a better eye on him when he did not feel well. Inside, though, I knew he was not taken from me.

Of all the loss I had sustained up to this point, this one left me torn in two and aching inside. His absence was a living thing, a monster that crept after me all hours of the day and night. I found myself talking to him in the dark, only to remember after a few words that I was well and truly alone. This feeling was different than what I had right after the crash, a hollowing of spirit that caused me to dissolve into fits of utter desolation. It took weeks before I let my heart form a thin shell around the gaping hole left by my brown and white companion, walling off the agony of his departure from my constant scrutiny.

Late that summer, drought descended, drying my waterfall to cracking mud and chipping away at the edges of my little pool until it was only a few feet wide and barely knee-deep in the center. I shared it with all the animals who ventured nearer now that they did not smell the dog. I woke one morning to Henry lapping away just outside the mouth of the cave, his tawny coat gleaming under the baking sun. I did not move an inch until he had his fill and sauntered off into the heart of his kingdom, tail flicking and whiskers dripping.

Even the river below, once wide and rushing, was a thin streak through the crispy foliage. After a night of thunder and lightning that did not produce so much as a single dribble of cooling rain, a new smell arrived on the wind. The mountain began to burn. Thick, choking soot and smoke hung in the air, leaving the sky dark all day long. The wildlife I shared my little puddle with ran, flew, and wiggled their way down the mountain and away from the heaviest smoke. Even the alligators abandoned their once marshy land, crawling on their bellies through the dry brush toward where the river used to rush past. I kept close to the cave while critters of all kinds marched past. A black bear, raccoons, a herd of wild boar, all of them tramped along the water's edge, stopping for a quick sip as they sniffed the air, then continued down.

I watched planes float above, dropping blankets of red dust onto the distant flames that crept closer and closer. The nights were lit in an eerie orange glow. Sometimes, glowing embers would drift from the sky like fireflies, puffing out breaths of smoke when they hit the dry leaves on the ground. I regretted not following the rest of my furry and feather neighbors off the mountain. It felt like years filled with smoky dark hours as I took to hiding in the deepest part of the cave, but it was probably only a few days before the first good rain fell.

The waterfall was the first sign that things were changing. A night of slow, steady rain turned the dry waterway into a drip, then a trickle, then a full stream cascading from above by the time I opened my eyes in the morning. The cracking mud became a soupy mess, sticking to everything, and burned patches of forest speckled the landscape. The air smelled fresh again, cooling the ache in my throat. Within days of that first rain, new shoots of grass poked out of the ground, and the sounds of birds took up full force. It was a short-lived blooming. The dryness was not done with the mountains yet.

Fall charged in before I could even wrap my head around the devastation the fires had left behind. It brought cooler temperatures and some much-needed rain, but the worst of the drought continued through autumn, through an unseasonable warm winter, until I could not tell one season from another. I was hungry in the dry forest, but more than that, I was *bored*. This new feeling was like an itch between my shoulder blades that I couldn't quite reach. In the coldest stretch of winter, I would daydream staring in the wavering firelight. Long-forgotten memories surfaced, bringing with them the ghost of sounds, tastes, and smells I could never quite grasp ahold of. One of the most potent was the smell of salty water and sunbaked boardwalk:

My parents and I were in Florida after a long, long drive from Pennsylvania. The sand was clean and white, almost like snow, and the water clear enough to see little fish darting around. We walked for hours, picking up seashells and sand dollars, staring into tiny tide pools filled with life, and racing sand crabs to their burrows. We got slushies and soft pretzels on the pier, sharing with greedy seagulls and laughing as they swooped around us.

It was one of the few memories I had of my father.

Fingers of loneliness tightened around my heart. It wasn't just the cave that echoed my voice but the valleys and the mountains themselves, tossing my frustrated screams over treetops and teasing me with its fading return. Why now, I thought, why did the loneliness find me now? Spring answered the echoes in sheets and torrents of rain, drowning the dry, crackling leaves.

My pool grew, swallowing up the ground, raging down to the river that swelled, spilling over its banks and gobbling up everything in its path. The waterfall became a thing of danger, reaching out to grab me as I crept over the slick rocks, and when I fell in, it pushed me into the roiling water, holding me fast to the silt below as I clawed uselessly for air and freedom. I pulled myself along the bottom until I was loosed from the sucking force.

One unusually fine day between downpours gave me an opportunity to wander the soggy mountain and replenish my ever-dwindling food supply. I found more mushrooms than I had ever seen, a carpet of them in some places, and stuffed myself to the brim in the bright sunshine of afternoon. As I popped them into my mouth, I thought back to Jack leaning his forehead on the seat in front of him, gazing at the leaves in the window. Threads of his voice dangled in my ears, asking me what the forest was saying. I turned a full circle, looking at the new growth and listening to the birds. The forest was happy again, full of life and water. It was singing.

I strolled along the high creek far below the falls when something caught my attention. A gleaming white lump stuck out of the mud at the water's edge. I brushed away the thick mud, uncovering a skull and a few other bones. A small handful of red and white fur clung to a shred of leathery-looking skin glued fast to a few ribs. Biscuit. I tossed down the skull in horror, stripped of every single feeling but the gnawing ache of his loss. This wasn't really Biscuit, just his bones. Biscuit, the wise old dog who'd kept me safe, deserved more than an unmarked grave of sucking mud on the bank of the creek.

I pulled back my shoulders and looked blindly into the sun, bracing myself for what I was about to do. One by one, I picked up all the bones I could find, washing the mud off in the rushing water. I carried them to the only place that seemed fitting, the place my mother had died, amongst the wreckage of the burned-out plane.

The clearing was strange, wilder than it had been the last time I'd visited. It had been spared by the fires for some reason I could not fathom, and yet, the trees still carried scars and burns from the crash. I sat with my pile of bones, miserable amongst what little remained of the twisted metal plane. Here was a place I had learned to avoid, skirting the edges, averting my gaze, as if that would make it go away. It felt like a cathedral or a cemetery or an abandoned castle, wide and empty, haunted, hidden from the world. There was a hollowness in the air, like all the oxygen had been sucked away, leaving me breathless and exhausted.

At the very edge of the clearing, I dug the hole with my bare, shaking hands, sifting through the loose, pebbly soil, and laid Biscuit to rest.

CHAPTER FOUR

I grew taller, bronzer, and less content as the months hopped over one another. The softness of childhood fell away, and in its place grew muscle. Things I had struggled with only a season or two before felt like mundane tasks that just filled the void of time. Finding food became less of an obsession and more of a chore, though I did heed the old man's warning and kept drinking the pine needle tea daily. It was bitter since I had run out of honey. I spent as much time lying on fallen logs staring up into the empty sky as I did foraging. Without anyone, without Biscuit, days just blurred one into the next.

In my sixteenth summer, I spent huge swaths of the hot days lounging outside the cave on a well-shaded, wide, flat rock with my feet dangling in the warm water. On a particularly blistering day, when the sun felt like fire and the air was thick and heavy, I thought I was dying.

My belly cramped, and my back ached, and when I stood from the rock, I was shocked to see blood on the dull gray surface. I looked down to find a thin trickle on the inside of my leg and panicked. For the briefest of moments, I imagined I had been bitten by something while I'd napped. Panic rose in my throat as I reached down to find what horrible wound might be there. When I could find nothing other than my regular bits and pieces, it finally occurred to me what was going on. I could hear the memory of my mother's voice whispering to me about the things that happened to young women as they grew up. I did not remember her saying how awful it would feel, though.

It took four months before the appearance of blood no longer sent me into fits of panic. It wasn't as though I could hide in my cave and bleed privately for a few days at a time, so I learned to ignore the discomfort and mess.

Some days, I looked at myself in complete confusion. My arms and legs felt too long to control. I would run through the forest and trip over my own feet as if I had never used them before. My fingertips reached branches that once seemed impossibly high. The unruly hair that grew in tangles down my back frustrated me no end. It would catch in the briars no matter how much effort I put into keeping the tangles out. One afternoon, I had lost my patience and used the dull little knife to cut away the worst of it, leaving it just at my shoulders. I left the long blond strands outside and watched the birds carry them away to make their nests.

Unfortunately, even the well-etched muscles could not shield me from the feeling of loneliness that started breaking free of the walls I had created. I missed my mother, Jack, and the old man terribly, but most of all, I missed Biscuit. He had been so deeply enmeshed in my life on the mountain that I hardly recognized my own shadow without his.

I found myself creeping about the woods, spying on anyone who happened to stumble into my wide-ranging empire. I trusted no one after my encounter with the men and their rifles, yet for some reason, I could not leave well enough alone and avoid people altogether. More of them traipsed about in Henry's kingdom, stirring up the big cat. I saw his tracks in unfamiliar places, his leftovers chewed but barely covered, and caught glimpses of his restless prowling more and more.

With excitement pounding in my heart, I would sneak into camps at the darkest hours, creeping on silent feet over the carpet of fallen needles, and stand inches from where the people slept. If I found a camp filled with the mess of inconsiderate litterbugs, I emptied the coolers they'd tied up in trees and take the food deep into the woods to leave as an offering for the animals that shared the forest. I collected the trash and filled up their coolers with it, disgusted that they had such little regard for the mountains that they left their wrappers and cans wherever they fell. Often, when they awoke, they abandoned their camps in a rush, exclaiming over the unwitnessed events. As I watched new sets of adventurers pack their things the morning after, I heard them talking about how Bigfoot had stolen their stuff. I looked at my not very big feet and smiled, thinking how disappointed they would be to know who was really behind it all.

Summer baked the mountain dry once more, and the flow of campers slowed to a trickle, just like the little falls. The berries shriveled on their branches, and even the mushrooms seemed to melt away, but it was not as bad as the last drought. I still crunched through the woods on crackling kindling with worry in my heart, knowing it would not take much to light up the whole world with fire once more.

As the red sun rose, leaving shimmering waves on the ground already at dawn, I heard the sound of dogs barking far off. I was torn between the deep desire to run toward the barks and apprehension about what I would find if I did. No amount of worry could keep me from walking away from the safety of my cave that day. I followed the echoes on trails I had not walked in ages. They led me in a familiar direction, toward the rotted cabin where I'd first met the old man.

The grass in the clearing had wilted in the heat, leaving dusty patches and weeds to speckle the expanse from the trees to the cabin. As I peeked around a thick tree trunk, I was shocked to see a group of hikers standing near the collapsed porch. A trio of black and brown dogs milled at their feet.

A man walked around from the opposite side of the cabin shaking his head. "Not good, guys, not good. Looks like we've got to call the forest service or the police or something. There's a dead body in there." He pulled something out of his pocket and turned away. "Ah, damn. No signal."

"Oh my God, really? Should we, like, cover it up or something till they get here?" A small woman in a pair of bright purple shorts rocked back and forth on her toes.

"Steph, you can't mess with evidence like that," another replied.

One of the dogs tilted its head and looked in my direction.

"Evidence? Like, murder or something?"

"Calm down, Nancy Grace. Nobody was murdered. Its lying in a bed and probably has been for a long time from the looks of it. Let's head back to camp and see if we can call someone. Nothing has bothered it for this long, so it's pretty safe to assume it'll be there once the authorities get here."

The group all started talking at once, ignoring the dog who had taken a few steps toward my hiding place. I could see his tail rising, along with the fur on his back, and my hands twitched in their desire to smooth it down.

"Java. Heel." The dog froze, then turned and walked back to sit next to a man with a walking stick, looking back a few times.

"Well, before we go, I want to have a look around." Another man walked to the back of the cabin, ignoring the complaints of his friends. He was only gone for a few minutes and reappeared with the old man's rifle in his hand.

"Put that back, dude. It's not yours to take."

"Whatever. He ain't using it anymore. Besides, it's a rusted-out piece of junk. Wouldn't even shoot, I bet."

"So why do you want it?"

"'Cause it's cool."

"I'm not kidding, man, put it back. I'm not staying out in the same woods where you stole from a dead guy. This is some *Blair Witch* level stuff, and I have no interest in finding out if ghosts can seek revenge."

"Don't be such a pussy, man. Ghosts aren't real, and neither was that stupid movie."

"Yeah, well...either way, put it back. Seriously."

The argument continued for a few minutes, but the gun thief held his ground. Soon, they all walked off down a game trail, chattering loudly about their discovery and the history of the rusty rifle. I could not bring myself to go see the old man, so instead, I walked out and sat on the pile of wood that had once been his porch. I stayed there even in the dark, slapping mosquitos and sweating.

A loud buzzing woke me from my terrifying dreams. I ran headlong into the trees almost before my eyes had fully opened, managing to hide as a pack of noisy machines rattled into the clearing. The men who jumped off all wore the same uniform except one, who carried a long board and a briefcase that said *Medical Examiner's Office* in bold white letters. They picked their way through the debris and into the cabin without speaking to one another.

They were out of sight for a long time before they came out carrying a yellow bag on the board. As they strapped it fast to one of the four-wheelers, the walkie-talkies began to buzz with static and muffled voices.

"Sorry. Repeat that, Marv."

The radio came to life again, and the men traded looks of surprise.

"You're telling me the same kids who found this guy found a downed plane, too? Unbelievable...Well, shit." All the men gathered closer, pulling out notebooks.

"Private plane or what? Not much left, then...Yeah, get on the horn to the NTSB, and we'll head on over to scout it out...Sounds like not much for us to do but wait...Ten four."

"Gonna be a long day, huh, chief?""

"Looks to be. But we don't have far to go for the next one. Looks like a few miles west and we'll be on scene. Jeff, you escort Claire back down with the body and wait for the feds to call. Might need to show 'em the way if they come out today."

Three four-wheelers headed through the woods, and the other two turned and disappeared into the trees. There was no way I could keep up, but I knew the woods and the trails far better than these strangers, so it took them longer to make it to the plane. The uniformed officers weren't there long, and when they left, I was reeling at the idea that the hidden plane had finally been discovered.

Was this what Jack had wanted, for this place to be found? For me to be found? Was this the answer to my restlessness since Biscuit had died? I sat at the edge of my little pool and wallowed in a new depth of misery. Since there was no one who loved me left on earth, where would they take me if I went to them? The old man had entrusted me with this wild place, and I could not bear to think of abandoning it to the hunters.

Within a few days of the initial visit, the police were back with a team of ball-capped people in jackets that read NTSB. They swarmed the crash site at the earliest light, shaking off the cold rain that smelled of autumn. For days, it drizzled while I peered through the glossy green leaves at the crew who picked over the crash site, scratching out notes in their notebooks.

They took pictures, drew sketches, measured everything carefully without ever looking up at me, the wisp in the trees, flitting around in their periphery like a woodland ghost. A crew of brawny men with ropes and sleds stripped the site bare of the remaining pieces of plane, whisking away their bounty on four-wheelers that left huge ruts in the growing mud. The largest parts were pulled into the sky by helicopter, blades screaming and disturbing everything for miles.

When they abandoned their task several days later, nothing was left but footprints, tire tracks, and empty space. Even the saplings that had taken root near the plane were trampled and uprooted. I walked through the clearing in a state of shock after they drove away, deafened by the sudden quietness. It felt as if a piece of me had been removed, an arm or a leg maybe, or something vital that I could not live without. Why hadn't I just walked out to them and said, *here I am, take me with you*? What weirdness had kept me hidden in the shadows of the woods while they'd worked? I didn't know what I wanted anymore. I didn't know who I was or where I belonged.

I spent weeks in a funk, tracing my steps to the cabin and the crash site daily to mourn the refreshed loss of those I had loved. It gnawed at me day and night. The seemingly endless cold drizzle of fall fueled my discontent.

When the sun finally broke through, it brought with it a tentative sense of ease once again. The woods around me came to life in the warm glow. It felt like summer again after so long in the cold damp air. The birds went wild in the trees, singing their hearts out overhead. A tender shoot of hope began to grow within me as I walked toward the empty clearing. I was so lost in the deep well of my new peacefulness that I stepped out between the trees and tripped over a thin string, narrowly avoiding crashing down on top of the tent in front of me. I froze, staring in surprise. This hadn't been here the day before. I crouched low, conscious that a tent meant a person, and if that person was close by, the last thing I wanted to do was to be caught unaware. I backed into the tree line silently, scanning the area.

A woman stepped out at the other side of the clearing, probably drawn by the sound of my clumsiness. She walked to her tent and held up the stake I had dislodged, turning it over in her hands as she looked around. There was something almost familiar about her, a memory that tickled the depths of my mind but could not be caught. She was tall and graceful, looking more at ease in the forest than anyone else I had seen on the mountain. Usually, the campers were loud and careless, almost rowdy amongst the quietness of their surroundings, but this woman walked with the confident strides of a mountain lion.

This was the first time I had ever seen a lone person. She crawled into the tent for a few minutes, backing out with a handful of gear. After another glance into the woods, she started right toward me. Horrified and fascinated at the same time, I backed away, hiding in the brush, afraid my pounding heart could be heard for miles. She looped something around the trunk of the tree a few feet away, then moved off to the left. After a while, she reappeared in the clearing and dragged more equipment out of her tent. She laid it all out on a tarp and began a slow, measured walk of the clearing. I stayed hidden in the tree line, watching her work.

She spent hours at the crash site in the daylight, sifting through the forest floor meticulously. The heat grew, and she stripped to her tank top, mopping the sweat off her face with a little towel. I watched her closely, wary of her sharp eyes drifting along the line of brush that camouflaged me. She had her long dark hair braided neatly down her back and broad, freckled shoulders tight with muscle. Still, that feeling of familiarity persisted as I watched her. I felt a confusing mix of emotions that I could not identify, a yearning to step into the light to say hello. I looked at myself in dismay, for the first time considering how bad I looked. What would she think of me, dirty and naked, chipped tooth and ratty hair? Probably run screaming like I was the boogie man. I slipped a little farther into the brush, more confused than ever as she worked on, oblivious.

She set up strings like a grid over the ground, laying everything she unearthed on the big silver tarp. I could not help but notice her hands as she ran her fingers along the items she found. They looked strong and capable, bigger than my own. I wondered if they were calloused or soft. My own felt rough, like tree bark, nothing like the soft hands of my mother. I rubbed my palms together and wiggled fingers that looked so thin compared to hers. I caught myself creeping closer as I studied her.

Despite my confusing desire to be near her, I kept my distance until darkness fell. When she lit a small fire and rested on a log, I inched nearer than I had been all day. She was humming softly, tapping her foot in the leaves as she drank a bottle of water. I had forgotten all about the odd box she'd strapped to the tree until I walked close to it, and a red light flashed. It startled me enough that I nearly fell into a briar bush.

Once more, my clumsy fumbling drew the attention of the woman by the fire. The beam of her flashlight swept over the area in wide arcs. I ducked behind a thick pine tree, holding my breath. The light passed by me a few times before I heard the quiet rustle of her returning to her seat. I carefully slipped into the deep dark forest and headed back to the cave.

After a sleepless night, I dragged my tired body outside and bathed in the icy water of the little pool, combing out my shaggy hair as best I could. Though I was still undecided about showing myself to the fascinating stranger, I figured there was no harm in looking more like a regular person and less like a muddy toad. I stood in the cave, wide awake and cleaner than I had been in a long time, staring at the suitcase that held my mother's clothes. I opened the top and pulled out a summer dress. The pale pink fabric was splattered with huge white flowers and tangled green vines. It would fit me now that I was taller, but I could not bring myself to slide it over my head. The faint smell of my mother's perfume was haunting and filled me with despair. I folded it up and gently placed it back in the suitcase. Instead, I took a torn flannel shirt, the only one not shredded to tatters, and slipped the huge thing over my thin shoulders. It hung low, but with the sleeves folded up a few times, it was easier to manage. The buttons had long since been lost, so I tied a string around my waist to hold it closed.

My steps were light and quick down the narrow trails to the crash site. Every yard I traveled closer had my insides twisted with excitement and terror. This was a new day, a new world, even, one that split me open like a bolt of lightning and left me dazzled by possibility. I daydreamed about how the woman would smile and greet me, inviting me to share her fire while she told me all about the things she'd found. Before long, I found myself at the edge of the tree line near where she was bent over. When she lifted her hand from the dirt, my heart dropped clear to my heels. Biscuit. His skull rested on her palm, stained yellow by the soil but still recognizable.

I was furious. What right did she have to take Biscuit from his spot? She laid the skull on her tarp and went back to work, but I did not stay to watch her. I returned that night, intent on taking the skull back. In a fit of bravery, I stole through the darkness, almost into the ring of light made by her fire and snatched up the skull. Relief washed over me as I covered it once more, returning it to its rightful place in the earth. I watched her for hours, long after she doused the fire and crawled into the tent. When the zipper sounded at dawn, I was lying in the branches overhead. It did not take her long to see the skull was missing. What I had not considered was the faint tracks I had left in the dirt.

"What the..." She knelt near the tarp and traced a finger along the edge of my footprint.

From my perch, I could see the trail of them clearly, leading right back to the place where Biscuit was buried. They must have been just as visible from the ground because she followed them, uncovering the skull once more with a look of surprise. She sat back on her haunches and turned her intense gaze to the forest. For what seemed like hours, she scanned the tree line and walked up and down as if looking for more footprints. She passed right by where I crouched, only a few feet away, close enough that I could smell the tang of her sweat and see the tendrils of hair escaping the slowly loosening braid. Everything about her spoke to a deeper part of me, something hidden and familiar, but I could not begin to place the emotion or the turmoil her presence evoked: fear of being discovered, fear of not being discovered, fear of all the other unknowns I was drowning in, different feelings that were gnawing at my midsection.

"Whoever you are," she called into the trees, "I'm sorry. I won't bother it again."

The woman spent the next few days sifting through the crash site, giving the area where Biscuit's skull lay a wide berth, taking long moments to stare into the trees. I watched her bite into the tough skin of an apple as she sat on a fallen log, close enough that I heard the crunch of her teeth through its fragrant flesh and close enough that I could see drips of sweat trickling down the side of her neck onto the dirt-stained tank top. Compelled to be near her, I slept in the tree overlooking her tent, rising and disappearing before she pulled back the flap to stretch in the morning light. At night, I stood at the edge of her firelight in the darkness, just out of sight, squirming against the desire to step into the glow of the flames.

She seemed sad, her eyes always searching the ground and the corners of her mouth tight. There were moments where she would get very still, tilt her face upward, and let the tense muscles of her shoulders relax. Six days from her arrival, the tarp, tools, tent, and small pile of treasures she had uncovered were zipped into a tall pack. She made a tiny fire that night, sleeping next to it under the dark, starry sky. When her breathing was slow and deep, I crept out of my hiding place.

She looked younger in her sleep, content and happy, with just a hint of a smile pulling at her lips. Her skin was smudged with a fine layer of dirt that almost matched the depth of her tan. Freckles, smaller than the ones on her shoulders, dusted the ridge of her cheekbones, and the frizz of dark hair that escaped her braid looked as dense and wild as the underbrush of the forest. I was close enough to see the gentle flare of her nostrils as she breathed, close enough to brush my hand along the wisps of hair that moved in the soft breeze, close enough to watch the steady beat of her pulse at her throat. I sat there for a long while, my emotions at war over what to do. She felt like an old friend, familiar and kind, but I really didn't know her at all. She was not like the others, who left their trash and took what they could from the forest. Could I really trust her, though?

Dawn was rapidly approaching, so I climbed up into my tree and rested. When I opened my eyes, the sunlight had barely begun to peep through the leaves. As suddenly as she had arrived on the mountain, she was gone. It happened so quickly, I nearly missed it. She rolled up her blanket, smudged out the little fire ring, and walked into the trees. Part of me longed to follow her down whatever trail she was taking, no matter the destination. Indecision paralyzed me as I stretched across the thick branch, straining to see the flash of color of her overstuffed backpack.

What she left behind was the silence I had once loved. For days, I went back to the clearing and stepped in her faint footprints, traced the ground where her tent had perched, looked for some other sign of her presence. Nothing remained but divots in the dirt. When they washed away, I had only memories.

I felt more alone than I'd ever thought possible. The strange emptiness that had been following me for months finally swallowed me, leaving me restless and unhappy. I managed to push the encounter out of my mind after a few weeks, following other campers who wandered into my territory, listening to them chatter in fits and starts. Sometimes, I would hear them talking about the old man or the plane crash, laughing and making things up as though they knew what had really happened. They spread rumors with well-practiced confidence, spouting theories, telling ghost stories. I began to hover at night to listen to them talk around their fires, wondering what it would be like to step out and join them, to tell them the truth about everything. Just the thought made my stomach roil with fear.

They were so different from the woman at the clearing, wearing their brand-new outfits and thick-soled shoes, and cooking exotic-smelling foods. I was a stranger to their world, an interloper who clung to my privacy with both fists. They were loud and rowdy, out of place in the quiet of the mountains.

Winter fell again, settling in stubbornly with a bitter wind that snapped dead limbs off trees and drove visitors away. I set my trap, made my rounds, sheltered in my lonely home. The vast emptiness I faced wore me down when winter reached out its frostiest fingers to clutch at my body. It seemed an eternity until the crisp mornings gave way to warmth, waking the forest from its slumber.

On one exceptionally fine spring morning, I basked in the sun on the rocks outside my front door, content to just exist in the moment. I was startled into alertness as the brush nearby rattled with life. Sitting stock still, I waited to catch sight of whatever was stalking about. Out from the undergrowth rolled a pair of tiny tawny kittens, tussling energetically. Behind them, with a chuff of admonishment, strode Henry. I had spent so long thinking of him as a *him*, as a king, that I'd never considered he could actually be a *she*. One more kitten pounced through the foliage after her, colliding with its siblings and adding to the pile of chaos beside the pool. The big cat stood regally next to her progeny, turning her golden eyes to me in challenge. There was a moment when I thought she would charge, the hair on the back of my neck whipping to attention, but she did not.

They drank, lapping politely at the water, then vanished amongst the weeds, leaving me trembling in their wake, fully changed by what I had witnessed. I'd never considered that our uneasy truce would see me only a few feet away from such an incredible event. Ashamed, I thought back to the times I had stolen from her. What if she had been feeding babies, and I'd taken what they'd needed? Henry, who'd saved us as we'd starved that brutal winter, was so much more than I could have imagined. I looked for her every day, hoping to catch sight of the adorable kittens, but she was so elusive, I only glimpsed them once more in the months that followed, just a flash of gold through the briars that left me wondering if it was really them at all.

CHAPTER FIVE

The next two years passed in much the same manner, hunger and fulfillment my only priorities, but toward the end of my nineteenth year, the grinding of days and months against one another left me careless and tired, oblivious to the dangers I'd once feared with every step.

The day started out innocently enough, heavy with humidity, electricity dancing in the volatile air of mid-spring. Lightning flashed in the distance, far enough away that I was unconcerned. I wandered through my domain with a practiced step, down to the river, then back up into the wood, past the crash site, past the cabin, high into the wildest part of the Ozarks, where I had set a simple wire trap to snag a passing rabbit. As I knelt in the thick bed of decomposing leaves, I caught a flash out of the corner of my eye.

The strike happened quicker than I could react, a thump against my leg that felt like a bee sting. My brain barely had time to consider what had happened when I reached down to touch the stinging as the culprit slithered away along the forest floor. With growing horror, I watched the cottonmouth retreat, disappearing amongst the leaves and branches. The two small puncture wounds welled with blood on the back of my calf, now burning like I had dropped hot coals on the surrounding flesh.

I sat on the damp ground on the verge of hysteria, trying to figure out exactly what to do. The old man had warned me of snakes, and I was always careful, always checking. He told me how a snakebite could kill, what to watch out for, all the ways a fool could die on the mountain, and now, *I* was that fool.

Desperately, I tried to remember what he'd told me about treating the wound. The story he'd told of his brother's death leapt into my thoughts. I was going to die just like his little brother. I could feel the bile rising in my throat as the realization dawned that I needed help. I sat, wallowing in misery as I thought of my mother for the first time in ages, crying for her, for all the other losses I had endured, crying for my own stupidity, my carelessness, how one choice, one measly second, could change everything.

I raced down the mountain—the burning feeling creeping out in waves from the bite—and careened across the rocks into my cave. I snatched up two of my most treasured items from my meager possessions and took off once more, heading for the nearest campground. Time slowed, everything happening in slow motion, like the day I had been sucked under the falls after a massive storm. This time, as I clawed my way through the woods, there was no surface to break through, no relief for my aching lungs, no shimmering surface within sight. It took more and more effort to close the distance, my feet acting as though they had doubled in weight every few steps from the tonnage of my fear, and the adrenaline coursing through me.

By the time I reached the edge of the tree line that surrounded the clearing, I was only aware of the direction I was headed, nothing else. As blackness overtook me, the only thing swimming in my vision was a young man, face etched with concern as he leaned over me. I could hear him shouting, feel the warmth of his hands on my shoulders, sense the nearness of others. I weaved in and out of awareness, not long enough to make sense of anything that was happening, but the air around me was pulsing with activity. I lifted my head off the ground despite the world tilting at the slightest movement and looked at the blue blanket draped over me. My swollen leg stuck out, wrapped in a white cloth.

"She's awake," the young man yelled. "Hey, lady, look at me. Keep your eyes open, okay?"

"They're sending a chopper. ETA seven minutes," another voice answered.

I rolled my eyes upward, meeting the stare of the first man who hovered over me. I was so tired from my run, thirsty, filled with regret.

"No, no, no. Don't close your eyes. Stay awake, honey…" The voice faded away as I drifted off to sleep.

I woke to the sound of thumping of helicopter blades overhead, grimacing in pain as I was lifted into a wide basket. Straps were tightened all around me, and I struggled against them as best I could. Air was rushing around me, and the ground fell away. I swayed in the harsh wind, unable to do more than stare at the underbelly of the helicopter growing larger and larger. Again, the blackness took over.

"Ma'am? Ma'am, can you hear me? Can you tell me your name?" A new voice broke through my dreams.

The bed beneath me dipped and swayed, the air filled with a roar of wind. A new level of panic settled over me, and I began swinging wildly, trying to grab ahold of something to help me sit up. My mind erupted with memories of the last time I had been into the sky. Hints of acrid smoke tickled the insides of my brain. More straps were fastened over my body, holding me firmly, and I couldn't seem to find a way to release them.

"Shit," a voice howled over the cacophony of blades whirling above us.

"You okay, Lance?"

"What the hell, man. *She broke my frigging nose.*"

"I got her, I got her. Go sit down."

The voices began to fade once more, and my body grew heavier and heavier, swallowed up by the darkness.

❖

My eyes were bleary when I tried to open them, taking their sweet time focusing on something other than the back of my eyelids. The astringent smells that assaulted my nostrils were all wrong, the feel of the cloth against my skin unnatural. It seemed that only minutes had passed since I was running through the forest, yet my senses rang with alarm that far more time had slipped from the clock. I rolled my head to the left, blinking rapidly to clear the fog. A machine beside me beeped gently, rhythmically. Cords of fluid stretched down, coursing into my veins. I pulled at my arms, my legs, but they were strapped tightly to the metal rails of the bed, holding me captive. I strained weakly against them, working hard to slip my hands or feet free to no avail. A whooshing sound arrested my movement, and the door slid open, admitting a heavy, scruffy-looking man in a white coat into my room. He checked the equipment, then pulled a metal folding chair to the side of my bed and sat.

"Hello, young lady. How are you feeling today? I'm Dr. Marcus." He reached out to pat my hand, and I flinched, making him draw away and lean back. "We're still trying to piece together what happened, but now that you're awake, maybe you can fill in the blanks for us."

He waited patiently in the creaking chair while I held my

tongue. I refused to meet his eyes, focusing on the yellowing tile overhead. I tested the straps once more, feeling just how much play they had.

"Okay, how about I start? You were admitted to the hospital with a venomous snake bite to your lower right leg. Upon arrival, you were unconscious, vitals weak, and exhibited localized edema. We administered several vials of antivenin over a few hours, stopping the spread of the toxin through your system, but your blood pressure and breathing were dropping into a non-life-sustaining range. You were intubated, placed on a ventilator, and sedated for your safety. The restraints were to keep you from pulling at the hoses or harming yourself. That was two days ago. This morning, your vital signs were looking good enough to extubate. However, when we began to lower the amount of sedation, you put up quite a struggle, so we decided to keep the restraints until you were fully awake."

He leaned forward and held a stethoscope to my chest. After nodding, he pointed to my bandaged leg.

"The wound is looking good, minimal edema, probably no permanent damage beyond a little scarring. You were very lucky. The admitting doctor says it is unlikely that you received a fully envenomated bite from the snake, probably just a warning bite with enough toxin in it to induce pain and swelling. Most of the symptoms you experienced may have been brought on by stress, shock, and exhaustion. A bit of rest and you'll be right as rain. That's about all we know. So can you fill me in on what led up to this?"

I closed my eyes, utterly overwhelmed by the smells and sounds of the hospital. My throat felt like I had eaten a handful of fire ants. Honestly, the rest of me didn't feel much better than that. I tried replaying in my head everything I could from the bite on, but it was just flickers of images that made no sense. I remembered that I'd had Jack's wallet and watch in my hand when I'd left my cave, and I needed to find them. The doctor waited, and minutes stretched on around my silence before he gave up peppering me with questions.

"Okay, then. I'll give you a little more time to adjust, and we can try again later." He walked out of the room, tapping on the little electronic box, perplexed expression on his face.

For the next three hours, I was alone in the overly white room, leaving me plenty of time to work on my escape. Keeping one eye on the door, I nearly dislocated my thumb before I managed to free one hand from the leather restraint, then set to work undoing the remaining three. I debated pulling at the cords that tethered me to the machine, but the first tug hurt enough that I abandoned the idea quickly. Instead, I searched as far as I could reach for my possessions, finding nothing but empty drawers and alcohol wipes. The whoosh of the door caught me sitting against the wall beside the bed, crying. A soft hand reached out, helped me to my feet and back into bed.

"It'll be okay, honey. The doctors are taking good care of you. You'll be good as new soon. Nice to see you up and about." She looked at the chafing on my wrist and clucked her tongue. "Awful things, aren't they? Barbaric. We'll get you a little cream and fix that right up. My name is Abigail. I'm one of the nurses taking care of you."

Her smile reminded me of my mother's, stretching wide across her face and showing all her teeth and gums. It even crinkled the skin at the corner of her eyes. She reached out and rubbed a section of my hair between her fingers, shaking her head.

"Let me just get the okay to get you in the shower, then I bet everything will start looking up." She tapped into her own little box, then fussed around the bed until a beep had her tapping again. "*Aha*. There we go. A shower it is. That all right with you?"

A shower? A real, hot water shower with soap and shampoo and no minnows nibbling on my toes? I didn't know whether to laugh or cry at the thought. Abigail waited until I gave a tiny nod, then unclipped me from the cords and held my arm as I wobbled weakly into the tiny bathroom. I stripped off the scratchy gown and stood under the warm flow of water. She used gentle hands to lather up my hair, bringing memories of my mother into sharp focus. I stood passively, allowing her to wash away years of grime and grit, a task that took nearly a half hour. Muddy brown water swirled down the drain at my feet. When the water was shut off, she spent time delicately picking apart my tangles until she could slide her fingers through without having them catch.

I slipped on a new hospital gown as she stripped the dirty linens from the bed and stretched fresh ones over the plastic mattress. Once I was lying down and hooked back up to all the little tubes with fresh bandages and soothing cream on my wrists, she stood back and clapped her hands.

"My Lord, it's like a whole new person lying there. What's a pretty little thing like you doing running around like a dirty heathen, playing with snakes? You aren't one of those religious folks that do all them crazy snake church services, are you? Nah. That can't be it at all. I heard the doctor say you won't talk to him," she nattered as she fussed with the sheets and pillows. "That's just fine with me, honey. You keep all your secrets, 'cause all talking does is make them start adding zeros on those bills piling up. Just press this little button here if you need anything at all. Don't you worry about being a bother, either. It'll save me from having to listen to those young nurses out there blabbing on and on about stuff nobody needs to know."

I tried a weak smile, using that to thank her for the care she had taken with me. She patted my cheek and grinned, broad and gleaming, as she tucked me in. She turned back and winked as she passed a new woman in a white coat in the doorway, then hurried out.

A regal-looking woman with high cheekbones and glossy black hair sat lightly on a rolling stool as she read my chart. I watched the smooth plane of her brow react with a lively dance as she scanned the papers, her toe bobbing in the air as she crossed her legs. The smile on her face did not reach her eyes, and I squirmed uncomfortably when her gaze met mine. Her eyebrows were sharp and intimidating.

"Hello, young lady. I'm Ana Oliveira, the social worker for the hospital. They've sent me in to find out a little bit more about you for our files. How are you feeling?"

She aimed a high-voltage smile at me, opening her palms as though she were trying to make sure I knew she was harmless. Her strong perfume hung in the air between us like a curtain, clouding my thoughts with memories of my mother:

The department store was huge, packed with people the week before Christmas. Workers flitted around filling racks and helping customers. We were on a mission to find the candy counter, my mother and I both craving their peanut butter fudge squares. Between us and the long aisle that led to our destination was the one thing we hated most of all, the perfume counter. My mother wiggled her eyebrows at me and grabbed my hand.

"One, two, three," she whispered. We ran past the counter through clouds of suffocating scents, laughing and gagging at the overpowering smell. Even after we were done shopping, the perfume clung to our clothes and seeped into the fabric

seats of the car. We pinched our noses shut and pretended to pass out before heading home with the little box of fudge resting on my lap.

Ana Oliveira wore one of *those* terrible perfumes. It was unnerving enough to make me shrink away, yet the memories it brought back were achingly joyful.

She tilted her head a bit. "It looks like you've gotten all the treatment you need, the swelling and redness are just about gone, and the bite wounds are closing nicely, according to your doctor. Since we didn't have any medical records, they did give you a tetanus shot to be on the safe side. We tried contacting the person whose wallet you were carrying, but he appears to be deceased. I did manage to get ahold of his next of kin, and she said she'll be flying down in a day or two to see if she can help us clear up the mystery here. It would be *really* helpful if you could point us in the right direction, though. Since the media is already sniffing around for a story, we've met to discuss releasing you, but this is kind of a strange situation. We want to make sure we have a safe place lined up for you where you can continue to get any treatment or support you need. We have many resources available, shelters and such, if you don't have a safe place to go to. Tomorrow morning, they're moving you to the third floor for observation until we can get some verifiable information on your identity. Anything you want to tell us before we start digging?" She leaned closer, raised her eyebrows, and said some words I didn't understand. "Okay, no Spanish or French. You certainly don't *look* Native American, but let's try Cherokee." Again, she made some odd noises and waited for me to respond.

I stared at her lips, watching her mouth move and studying her like she was an insect on a branch as she tried different languages to see if I would respond. I could see her color rising as she faced my stony silence. She began waving her hands around, making broad gestures. I had learned basic sign language when I was little because I hadn't talked much, so I recognized the phrase, "What is your name?" She also spelled out her own name slowly, letter by letter. After a minute or two, she sighed. She pulled out a board with various pictures on it and tried to get me to point to the things she asked about, like food or toilet.

"Okay, I get the feeling that you know exactly what I'm saying. Is there a reason you won't respond? I can see you looking at the correct picture when I describe it. Are you afraid to speak? No one here will hurt or judge you. If you're in some sort of trouble, we can find ways to help you. Have you been held against your will? We have an affiliated women's shelter for victims of domestic violence. I just need to know what sort of situation you're coming from so we can figure out where to place you. Do you use recreational drugs or alcohol?" She waited awhile for my response, then shrugged and headed for the door. "Suit yourself. I really am here to help. I want to make sure you get the kind of care you need."

She hesitated in the doorway, her back to me as though waiting for me to call out. She sighed again and departed, leaving me to brood in my self-imposed silence. I didn't know what to say. Would she have believed my story anyway? Talking was never my strong suit, and I was fighting the urge to hide inside myself, to curl up and shut out the rest of the world like I had long ago. Maybe if I squeezed my eyes shut long enough, I would open them up and be back at the edge of the little pool, squishing my toes in the warm, thick mud.

The smell of Ana's perfume lingered long after she left the room.

❖

Early the next morning, they transferred me from one room to another, smaller room on a different floor that had a locking wooden door. My IVs were pulled, the bandage removed from my leg, and I was given a gray shirt and a pair of cotton pants that I had to hold up with one hand when I stood. I had barely eaten, and my stomach growled in distress, but the food looked and tasted awful and sent me racing to the bathroom to vomit in the sparklingly clean flush toilet I had fallen in love with. I began to plan how I would bring it back to the woods with me so I could have the best of both worlds, my private playground and my porcelain throne.

When I stood and faced the sink, I was startled to see myself in the mirror. It had been years since I had seen a reflection, at least not one that wasn't wavering and incomplete in moving water. The person opposite me looked like a stranger. I reached up, touching the image that stared back in awe. My hair was thick and wheat-colored, curling and waving in frizzy wildness. My eyes were bluer than I remembered, reminding me of my mother's. Freckles congregated along my cheekbones and disappeared under my shirt. I was wholly different from the child who'd first stepped behind the waterfall. I was still gaunt and gangly, tall and narrow, corded with muscle. Everything about the woman in the mirror seemed alien, unfamiliar. If I squinted, it almost looked like a skinny version of my mother standing right in front of me. My heart squeezed painfully, and I turned away.

A few hours after I had settled in as best I could, there was a knock on my door, and yet another man in a white coat strolled into the room, clipboard in hand.

"Ma'am, I am Dr. Buchanan. It looks like you've healed up sufficiently, and your previous doctors agree that there isn't much more we can do for you here. Your chart says you are nonverbal and uncooperative in any other method of communication. I'm here to assess you and see if we can't set up a game plan to get you out of the hospital and into a safe living situation. I see we have no current address or family members on file." As he spoke, he looked at his chiming electronic box and pursed his lips. "Ah, I guess my assessment will have to wait a few minutes. Apparently, you have a visitor."

He shuffled me out the door, down a long hallway, to a well-lit room. He unlocked the door and ushered me in, pointing to the table and chairs in the center of the floor. I sat and waited for a while, alone, staring out the windows to the bustling urban sprawl below. It was culture shock, for sure, but nothing I didn't remember from my past. My mother and I had spent lots of time going places like Baltimore's Inner Harbor and the Smithsonian in DC as field trips to help with my lesson plans.

I couldn't explain why, but I felt like I didn't belong here, not with these people, not in this place. I watched people scurrying along the sidewalks and hopping in and out of taxis, convinced I was something entirely different from them, made of strange, unidentifiable parts. Those people below looked comfortable, happy even, waving and chatting with one another. I had never been a part of that world.

I heard the lock click, felt the blast of cold air from the open door, the sound of footsteps on the tile floor, the screeching scrape as the chair across from me was pulled out. I didn't turn my head right away, sure there would be a new doctor or another stranger waiting for answers that I couldn't give them.

"It was you, wasn't it? In the woods?"

My heart leapt into my throat, pulse racing as I whipped

my head around to look her full in the eyes. They were dark and voluminous, showing mixed emotions as she stared. I jerked to my feet, nearly upsetting the chair as my jaw dropped. Up close, I could see the resemblance, and the tantalizing memories that had swirled at the crash site finally clicked into focus. She looked so much like her father, more so now that she was dressed in slacks and a silk shirt instead of the tank top and faded jeans she'd worn on the mountain.

"Jessica." The name tripped off my lips and fell to the floor between us, a barely audible echo of my thoughts that bounced softly in the space between us. With that one word, my entire world tilted wildly. Sorrow welled in my eyes, threatening to spill over. I knew if I let it, it would fill the room and drown us both.

"How do you know my name? They said you couldn't talk. The administration called me because you came out of the woods with my father's wallet. How did you get it? What do you know about the crash? Have you been up in the woods ever since I was there?"

Her voice got louder with every question until she was shouting and shaking, fists clenching and releasing. I swallowed, shrinking backward as I was overwhelmed by her tone. My body language must have given her pause because she closed her eyes and sucked in a few deep breaths.

"I'm sorry," she mumbled, taking a moment to calm herself. "I didn't mean to yell. I just…I just need to know."

She smelled so familiar, the scent crackling through my memory to the day she'd passed my hiding spot. My mind swirled with all the things I wanted to say, but I could not seem to shake the dust off my voice to make them known. She paced back and forth by the window, still working her hands. Her long hair swung in a neat braid behind her, brushing across the back of her burgundy top. She pulled a creased printout from her back pocket and set it on the table before dropping heavily into the chair. It was a blurry black-and-white photo.

"My trail cam captured this, but I couldn't quite believe it at the time. You were there, spying on me, weren't you?" She tapped a finger on the photo and waited for me to respond.

It was definitely me, sticking out like a sore thumb in the dark underbrush. The shape of my body was a hazy, ghostly white, and my eyes reflected brightly.

"Who are you?" Jessica pulled something else from her back pocket then, setting Jack's wallet on the table next to the picture. I reached toward it, but she snatched it away.

"That's mine," I snapped, surprising us both. She looked at me with wide eyes, and I could feel the anger rising. This was mine, not hers. Jack had trusted me to take care of it. He would have been disappointed to know that I had been so careless.

"It is not. That belongs to my father."

"He gave it to me. It's *mine*." I made to grab it, but she held it up in the air, out of my grasp.

"*Bullshit*. My father died eight years ago. Tell me where you really got this."

I crossed my arms and threw myself into the chair opposite, glaring as she tucked the wallet back in her pocket. Had it really been eight years since the crash? No. That certainly wasn't right. Eight years was a lifetime. It felt like just a few summers ago when Jack had handed me his watch and sent me off to find water. How had so much time elapsed? I pinched my arm, trying to see if this was some sort of nightmare and not real life.

We sat in silence for a few more minutes, and then she jumped to her feet and headed for the door. Before I could stop her, she was gone, and in her place appeared an orderly who attempted to walk me back to my tiny room. The loss of her presence struck me like a train, flattening me, sitting on my chest like a boulder, stealing my breath. Soon, I was panting, gasping for what little air I could force in my lungs, my vision tunneling as I crumbled to the tile floor of the hallway. Large hands reached for me, grabbing, pulling, prodding me to rise, but I felt the life seeping from my pores and remained limp until unconsciousness overtook me. When I crawled my way back to awareness, there were three people standing over me, conversing as though I was a place mat on a dinner table.

"From what I heard, she scared the hell out of those campers when she burst out of the woods, naked and wailing like a banshee. I heard they had her doped up something fierce to keep her from tearin' her way out of the chopper."

"Yeah. I was there when the Versed started wearing off, and, man, she had four points and a chest strap that barely held. Kid's built like she's made of steel and dirt. Lance looks like he got hit by a bus. I bet his nose ain't *never* gonna be the same." There were a few snickers.

"They still don't have an ID? Heard they looked through missing persons, and there ain't a soul who matches her description. No dental matches, nothin'. What do you want to bet some dirty ol' bastard had her locked in his basement a few years?"

"Doc said she ain't said a word to nobody but that lady what showed up and set her off."

The voices faded in and out as I tried to shut down until my bladder finally pressed me into action. The room had cleared, and I tiptoed to the bathroom to avoid the duo who still chatted outside my door. When I looked in the mirror again, I thought back to Jessica and the changes that had come over her in the years since the picture Jack had carried. She was taller and more angular, every other feature a stronger version of her thirteen-year-old self. I could imagine her as the hiker from a few years ago, methodically searching for any trace of her father, sharp-eyed and intelligent as she scoured every inch of disturbed turf.

How had I not known who she was then? If I had, would I have made up my mind to walk out and greet her? Would my life still be my own instead of my being trapped inside this foul-smelling ward at the mercy of strangers, or would it all have led to this point anyway? I was still pondering, still looking into my own eyes as a commotion erupted in the hall outside.

A breathless Jessica barreled in, her presence leaching the oxygen from the small bathroom as she swelled to fill the doorway. "Tell me your name," she commanded, wild-eyed and gasping for breath. "Please. Tell me."

I could not resist the plea in her voice, the edge of chaos that bubbled up from her core. I tried once, twice, clearing my throat before anything could successfully emerge. "L…L… Lily."

"Jesus *fucking* Christ." The color drained from her face. "Did you just say *Lily*? As in Lily Andrews? Are you fucking kidding me? Lily?"

I nodded as much as I could manage in the face of her undoing.

She stepped backward, bumping into the door frame as she stared at me in shock. She was holding her breath as she bumbled into the sparse bedroom and let herself sink to the bed. Never once did she try to break eye contact, holding me prisoner to complex emotions she was grappling with. When I followed, leaning against the footboard, she tilted away from me with what I could only interpret as horror.

"This is not possible. You've got to be making this up. Where did you hear that name?" She put a hand out as if to reach for me, then snatched it back, looking at the digits as though it was impossible to fathom their traitorous behavior. She shook her head hard, dropping it into her hands as her shoulders trembled.

"I'm Lily," I repeated, my voice stronger. I was sure of very few things in the world anymore, but I knew without a doubt that I was Lily. "Jack gave me his watch to help me find water." I wasn't sure if she heard me. I stopped speaking, waiting for some signal that she wanted me to proceed.

The words were whispered so softly I nearly missed them. "Where is he?"

"Gone."

Her eyes were wells of sorrow, her face pinched with grief, and my heart broke for her. "When? Where? I don't understand."

"He couldn't get out. He told me what to do." This time, when her fingers brushed the sensitive skin on my forearm, she did not pull back. I could feel her struggling to make sense of what I had said. "He showed me your picture. The last day, he called me Jessica."

In clipped words, I began to relive the few days I had known her father, the way he'd taught me to survive, how he was generous and kind despite the circumstances, why he lost my name to hers at the end of our friendship. She cried racking sobs, fat tears coursing down her cheeks and splashing to the tiles as she hung her head low between her knees. I talked haltingly for an hour, undisturbed by the solitary man who took notes outside the door, listening as I started unfolding the map of my past. Jessica, gripped by a sadness darker than anything I had witnessed since my own when Biscuit had died, said nothing. When I reached the point at which her father called me by her name, she fled from the room.

CHAPTER SIX

For the next two days, I had doctor after doctor bustling about, taking blood, coaxing me to speak, desperately trying to prod me into revealing more. I endured it all in silence, broken by the idea that Jessica might never come back. There was not a soul left in this world who would understand what the mountain meant to me, the life that I had in the never-ending forest.

I wanted Abigail, the kind nurse who had used gentle hands and made me feel like a little girl again. I cried into my pillow, curling up in a ball beneath the sheets. I remembered her telling me to press the red button, and she would come, but when I did, it was another nurse who poked her head in the door.

"No. I want Abigail," I whispered as she came closer.

"Abigail who?" The nurse looked confused, so I pressed the button again and looked back toward the door. "Was Abigail downstairs with you?"

I nodded, then covered myself back up and turned away. It wasn't long before footsteps sounded next to the bed.

"Honey, what's the matter?" A hand tugged at the sheet, and when I looked up, Abigail was smiling broadly. "This sassy nurse called down and told me I needed to get my butt up here to cheer you up."

I flung my arms around her, clinging to her bulk for dear life. She smelled like the hospital soap, but her warmth seeped out of the soft material of her shirt as she held me close.

"Now, now. No need to cry about it. I'm here. Seems like you've got this whole hospital in a twist, honey. They've gone and shook things up downstairs so I can hang out with you for a little while. I'm betting a little TLC will wipe that frown right off your pretty face, won't it?"

The rest of the afternoon, she stayed in the room with me and chatted in a one-sided conversation, telling me about her children, her grandchildren, her ancient dachshund that piddled on the kitchen floor every time she came home after a long shift. She pushed me to bathe myself, fussed over the food served, and peppered me with inane questions about my favorite color or shape. Mostly, I listened, offering a smile or two, sometimes replying with a nod or a few words but wholly content just to have her nearby. When evening fell, she left me with promises that she would be back bright and early.

I felt a creeping sense of loneliness when they turned out the lights. The doctors had left my chart on a clipboard in the room, sticking out from beside a computer screen. I pulled it out, reading what I could of the bad handwriting and odd abbreviations. I fell asleep with it tucked under my pillow, still unable to decipher most of what was written.

Morning came quickly, and Abigail seemed to arrive with the first rays of sun through the big windows. I snapped awake at the sound of the door opening, relaxing when she appeared with a glass of apple juice.

"Whatcha got there, dear?" she asked, pointing to the edge of the clipboard sticking out. "Can you read that?"

"Some." I pointed to a few words I did not understand. "What is this word?"

She looked over my shoulder and shook her head. "You

don't want to know all that mumbo jumbo. That's just a whole lot of flapping gums trying to stick asinine labels on a person who hasn't a thing wrong with them. Not talking and not falling for all their crap just makes them want to stack more and more diagnoses in there so they can make use of all those fancy degrees. There's no need to worry about all that. They'll figure it out soon enough that you just need a little time. How about instead, we start getting you all dolled up, 'cause you got a big day today."

She pulled a thin cotton dress out of a bag and proceeded to make me as presentable as possible, brushing my unruly mane and fitting the new shoes she brought to my coarse feet. I was shocked and grateful when she pulled my bear tooth necklace out of her bag as well.

"Now, they had this little baggie with your ID number on it at the nurse's station, so I figured you might want it back. You just hide this under your dress, and it'll be our secret, okay?"

Her kindness brought tears to my eyes, and suddenly, in the face of all this change, I broke down. She wrapped her fleshy arms around me, rocking me on the bed like my mother used to do all those years ago, murmuring soothing words into my ear. When my sobs ebbed to sniffles and hiccups, she took my chin and held my face close to hers.

"You remember this, Lily. Not one person in this world is gonna fight for you the way you can fight for yourself. You are the strongest, bravest, most resilient person I've ever met, and don't you lose that, no matter what happens. There are big things in store for you as long as you don't let this greedy world eat you up. I got your back. If you ever need anything, you just call this number, and I'll round up the infantry." She slipped a small square of paper in my hand and gave it a squeeze.

"Are you leaving?"

"No, honey, but you are. Your grandmother, Dawn, is here to take you home."

I scrunched up my face, unsure how to react. I barely remembered my grandmother. We had visited her several times when I was very young, but our relationship was less family and more like related strangers. I remembered she had always been a frightening woman, hard and unsmiling. When we walked to the waiting room to greet her, the only familiar feature I could make out was the piercing blue eyes that looked a little bit like my mother's. I did not want to go with her and whispered as much to my Abigail.

"Not much choice, honey. You can't stay here forever, and your granny is pretty set on taking you back to Texas with her. The powers that be don't think you'll be safe if they just shove you out the front door and send you on your way. You turned out to be a pretty high-profile guest here in our little podunk town."

"No." I even surprised myself with the strength of my voice. "I don't know her."

Dawn arched an eyebrow, squeezing her thin lips together even tighter. "We've got your room all set up, Lily. You belong with us. Now, let's get a move on. It's a long drive from here."

She was my height, rail thin, and her hair was an unnatural shade of platinum. She stood as though steel rods held her straight. She was not jovial and kind like my mother had been, not quick with laughter or empathy. I felt no kinship here, just obligation, and that was enough to set my teeth on edge with distrust. I turned to Abigail and shook my head.

"Not many options here, honey. What is it you think we should do?"

"I want to go back to the mountain," I whispered in her ear.

"I'm pretty sure they aren't going to let that happen. That was state land, honey. There are a lot of unsavory characters who would be looking to take advantage of someone like you. You won't have to worry about that if you go with your grandmother. Considering your story has already brought in enough tourist revenue to repave Main Street, I bet the mayor would rather just put you in a cage and charge admission to any fool with wallet and a sick sense of morality. Best not to stick around here and find out, though." She *tut-tutted*, rubbing my back as she led me to a set of plush chairs.

Dawn crossed her arms, her face set in an expression that would have sent iron statues skittering to do her bidding. "No point in getting cozy. We've got to be going."

"Give her a little time to get used to the idea. All this new stuff to process can be a bit much, if you know what I mean. She only just found out about all this."

"Well, it isn't as though we have all day for her to gather the courage to do as she's told. All the paperwork is signed, and my car is waiting out front."

I could feel Abigail's anger at the oblivious, unmoved woman tapping her expensive-looking shoe on the tile floor. Her hand still rested possessively on my back, warm and soothing as I leaned into the pressure. Just when she opened her mouth to respond, another voice tickled my eardrums, prodding my heart into a full gallop.

"I have a proposition." Jessica was leaning against the door frame, one hand in the pocket of her slacks, as though she had been there for quite a while. "I've got a lot of unanswered questions, and I need to get some closure. I'm staying a few blocks away at the Holiday Inn. I'd be willing to take Lily with me for a few days, then drive her to Texas once I've picked her brain."

"And who exactly are you? I certainly don't think it would be appropriate to foist my granddaughter upon a stranger at such a delicate time. How do I know you aren't just here to exploit her for your own gains?" Dawn strode over to me and made a grab for my arm. I swatted her hand away and scrambled to my feet, crab-walking the few steps to Jessica.

"This is Jessica Velasquez," Abigail said, her voice measured and clipped. "Her father was on the plane. She was the only one to get Lily talking, and not that my opinion means anything, but I think it would be a great way to let her acclimate to being back amongst society by having someone her own age to confide in, don't you?" Abigail's question was hard-edged enough to send Dawn into a near tizzy of disapproving expressions.

"I don't rightly remember asking your opinion, *Nurse*," retorted Dawn, more than a hint of superiority seeping from her lips. "I am her family, not you, therefore, I am the one who has the responsibility of caring for her."

"Then I guess the only fly in the ointment is that Lily is old enough to make her own decisions. She's an adult in the eyes of the law," Jessica stated, crossing her arms to mirror Dawn's stance. "She's nineteen, right?"

"Why did this dreadful place drag me all the way across state lines to sign paperwork if I am not to concern myself with her well-being? I will *not* be leaving here without my granddaughter."

"Ma'am, when someone shows up to the hospital after being presumed dead for nearly a decade, it's a pretty safe bet that the closest family member will be notified as soon as possible. I'm not quite sure what the legal precedent is since I can't imagine this is a regular occurrence, but I'm willing to bet releasing Lily into the custody of a family member is all part of the 'cover your butt' clause in the hospital bylaws. We can keep her safe here, but once she walks out those front doors, all hell is going to break loose." Abigail's matter-of-fact answer felt like a lead weight hanging in the air as everyone stood quietly, looking back and forth. "Maybe we should ask Lily what she wants to do?"

All eyes turned to me, making me squirm. I waited a heartbeat, taking stock of my options. They would not allow me to go back to the home I had known for the last eight years. I would either be at the mercy of Dawn, Porcupine Queen of Texas, or Jessica, the person Jack had loved most of all. There was no contest. I pointed at Jessica, catching a sparkle of hope in her dark irises.

My grandmother pursed her lips, glaring at the three of us as though we had lured her here just to put a crimp in her busy schedule. "Fine. I will not force you to come if you truly wish otherwise. Your room will still be there next week. And you"—she pointed a bony finger at Jessica—"I will hold you one hundred percent responsible if something happens to this child while she is under your supervision." She turned away, but not before I noticed a wet gleam in the corner of her eye. Perhaps, under the unforgiving armor, something soft and human still lurked. Her exit took with it a great deal of the tension that had stifled us all.

Abigail leveled her sharp gaze on Jessica as if sizing her up. "I hate to agree with that old bag, but you better take good care of our girl. It's a whole different world out there."

"Of course." Jessica met my gaze and nodded. "You have my word."

Abigail called a taxi for us, even though the hotel was nearby, implying our walk would not be an easy one. I only realized why when she escorted us to the main entrance of the building, and we were accosted by journalists swarming the sidewalks.

"Miss Andrews, Miss Andrews," they all screamed over one another, stabbing cameras and microphones at me. "What was it like...How did you...This way."

All their words jumbled into a terrifying avalanche of noise. I whipped around and buried myself in the solid warmth of Jessica, who had been following closely out the double doors. I felt her stiffen, then relax into the pressure of my clutching arms, her own rising to shelter me from the buzzing reporters.

"Where did all these buzzards come from? None of them were here when I came in." Jessica held a hand in front of her face as she called to Abigail. If there was a response, it was lost in the rumble of the crowd.

Abigail waved, shushing the swarm backward as we aimed for the waiting taxi. The three of us tumbled in, slamming the door to fend off the growing noise. Our driver, apparently prepared for the chaos, pulled away from the curb smoothly, avoiding the reckless bystanders. We were silent as he drove, and the news trucks followed. The well-prepared driver headed for the nearest highway, weaving in and out of traffic, dodging slow vehicles. We drove for almost an hour just to make it to the Holiday Inn only four blocks from where we started. Not a soul waited for us there, all lost in the maze of the interstate, probably stalking some other poor taxi driver, mistaking him for ours.

Jessica and I climbed out of our cab, and I reached for Abigail's hand.

"I need to get back to work, Lily. I can't come with you."

"Why not?" Panic surged through me.

"You'll be fine, now, honey. Don't you worry." My terror must have been written all over my face because she reached up and held my cheeks gently. "She'll take good care of you. You still have my number, right?"

I nodded, holding out the crushed piece of paper I had been clutching since she'd handed it to me in the hospital. Then, as soon as the car door was shut, she was gone.

"Well, I suppose we better get you settled. My room is down here." Jessica pointed as we entered the front door. I followed closely, my feet clipping the back of her shoes and nearly sending her sprawling on the gaudy carpet.

"Sorry," I mumbled as she raised an eyebrow at me.

"Ah, it's fine. First day with my new feet," she said. If it was a joke, I didn't get it, and my lack of laughter led to an uncomfortable silence as she fished the key out of her pocket and opened the door. "Welcome to my humble abode."

I walked in, trying not to wrinkle my nose at the musty smell. It was more spacious than my room at the hospital, holding two full-size beds and a flat-screen TV. It was dark and cave-like, with window-length, room-darkening curtains and dim light bulbs.

"I guess we'll have to go out and get you a few things to wear. One dress isn't going to cut it." She sat at the table and flipped open her laptop, busily typing away.

I wandered around the room for a few minutes, touching various fabrics and running my hand along the varnished top of the dresser where the TV sat. I spent even more time in the bathroom, trying the handles of the faucets, reveling in the blistering hot water that gushed out. Hot water was amazing. I moved out into the room again, pulling back the curtains and looking at the view of the street. Far in the distance, mountains stretched along the horizon. Could that be where I had been for so long? If I walked out the door now, how long would it take until I found myself beneath the tall evergreens? I glanced back at the door, then to the mountains again.

"I was wondering," Jessica started, surprising me as I stood daydreaming, lost in my thoughts. "Would you be willing to show me where you stayed?"

I caught her eye, knowing her unasked questions about her father would be easier for her to voice in the mountains. "You'll take me back there?" The excitement rose, heating my cheeks and making my fingers twitch with longing.

"Sure. I mean, not to stay, but it won't hurt to visit, right? I'm sure you have some loose ends to tie up or whatever." Her feigned nonchalance did not match the nervousness in her tone. I knew she wanted to see what I saw, to know the place where her father had existed in his last moments. Her thirst for the past was matched by my own. Every moment I was gone from my cave, the memories seemed less and less real, as if it were a dream fading fast at my waking.

"I can bring stuff back here?"

"Of course. What sort of stuff?"

"My notebooks."

"Notebooks? You had notebooks up there? I guess I didn't realize you would have that sort of stuff."

"Uh-huh. A couple. I wrote almost every day until I didn't have any more paper."

"What sort of things did you write about?"

"Stuff I did, things I saw. Once I wrote about how much I wanted a hot dog. I thought about food a lot."

She grinned slightly. "I can totally relate to that. I would die if I had to give up pizza. I'm not sure if any of the fast-food joints around here sell hot dogs, but we could stop and see if you'd like."

I stared at her in wonder, realizing that I had completely forgotten the taste of my once favorite food. Would it even taste the same now? When I remembered my obsession, it brought back the sharp pangs of hunger, the weakness of starvation, the hours where I had lay on the dirt floor of my cave, waiting for death. It also brought back the smell of the big cat that had saved my life, the tang of pine needles and the cold bite of impending winter. I shuddered.

"Well, we'll take an extra backpack, and you can grab whatever you want. You have to promise me you won't run off, though."

I nodded half-heartedly, not really wanting to promise anything beyond this moment, still reeling from the train of my thoughts and the powerful emotions bubbling up.

She studied me a moment as if convincing herself it was a good idea to take me back to my mountain. "Okay. When do you want to go?"

"Now."

"Now? I think we're in for some thunderstorms in a few hours. Maybe we should wait until tomorrow."

It was my turn to arch a brow at her, trying out a tiny smile. "Are you scared of thunder?"

"Of course not. Thunder doesn't bother me at all. I'm just not thrilled with the thought of getting struck by lightning."

She blushed as my little smile grew. Warmth spread through my chest at the sight of her flushed cheeks. Our eyes locked for a moment, sending a tumble of confusing feelings rampaging through my thoughts. She looked away, visibly shrugging off whatever she had been thinking, and began to gather a few things into her backpack, which had been stowed in the closet. She tossed me a pair of her jeans.

"Can't go hiking in a dress, right?"

I put them on quickly, realizing I was both thinner and longer legged. Not wanting to spoil the mood, I tucked the dress into them, making the waist tight enough that they stayed put. When she glanced over, she covered her mouth as if to stifle a giggle.

I tossed her a questioning look, convinced I had missed yet another joke. Following the direction of her gaze, I looked at the inches of skin poking out below the denim hem. "Sorry," I mumbled sheepishly, pulling at them in a vain attempt to stretch the fabric down over my ankles. She leaned over and rolled them up, making me look a little more put together.

"That should do it. At least you have some decent sneakers. The going shouldn't be too tough in those." I looked at the nice white shoes I had and could not wait to shuck them from my unaccustomed feet. My toes itched to sink into the rich mountain soil once more.

CHAPTER SEVEN

We left through the front entrance and headed to her Subaru. When I opened the passenger door, the scent of her washed over me, intense in the midmorning sun. Her whole car smelled of the outdoors, flowers, and something unique I could not quite describe. I found myself desperate to name the familiar scent, scouring my memories for anything that might hold the key. It was so like the smell of her when I saw her in the woods, yet there was something else, something further back. I closed my eyes and allowed my senses to wade along the edges of the past until they reached a hidden memory.

The sound of Jack's wheezing filled my ears. He leaned to the right and reached into the depths of his pocket, struggling to extricate his wallet. When he finally handed it to me, the smell of the worn leather wafted up as I brushed my fingers over the butter-soft surface.

I turned in my seat, staring into the back of the Subaru at the piles of leather and brushes on the seat behind me. "What's that?"

Jessica looked over her shoulder after she started the engine. "Tack."

"What's tack?"

"For horses. That's a bridle, and my saddle is under the blanket there. Nothing fancy but it is comfortable and lightweight. Sorry it's such a mess in here. My car is kind of a my mobile tack room. Don't be surprised if a petrified carrot or two come rolling out from under the seat when I hit the brakes. One of these days, I'll get around to cleaning it out."

She shrugged, plucked a few short, white hairs from the side of my seat, then tossed them in the direction of the window. The slight breeze made them flutter back inside, down to the carpet at her feet to congregate with loose stalks of hay and dirt. I felt oddly at home amongst the chaos in her car, comfortable and centered, as though it was an extension of my mountain. Whether that came from the smell of leather and horses, the company of a familiar stranger, or the fact that we were going back to the safety of the woods, I could not tell.

She drove carefully through town, and after a while, the paved roads gave way to dirt and gravel, the pricey houses to aging farms.

"There's a Dairy Queen up ahead. Do you want me to stop for some hot dogs?"

I shook my head. My stomach was in knots at the thought of going home, and I didn't want to wait any longer. Soon enough, we were climbing, the potholes clawing at the car's tires and jostling us about. We crunched into the parking lot of the campsite closest to the place where I had been rescued. There was only one lonely car in the small gravel lot, a muddy Jeep with plastic windows. Jessica shouldered the huge pack she had brought to transport my things out of the cave as I tugged at the smaller backpack filled with snacks and drinks for our hike.

Despite the normal appearance of the forest, everything felt different. I wasn't sure if it was because of Jessica or if there was something about me that made everything feel strange. I could count on one hand how long I had been gone, but for some reason, it felt like years, like everything that had happened here could have been a memory or just a crazy dream. Even the fall of my feet on the ground felt oddly uncomfortable. I stopped and yanked the shoes off, at once feeling more connected to the ground. I sighed as my toes brushed against cool, squishy moss and stiff pine needles. This was my home.

"I want to go back to where the plane went down. Do you mind?"

"It's that way," I answered, pointing toward the west.

She nodded, then seemed to notice the shoes hanging from my backpack. "Uh." She looked at her own feet, then back to me. "You don't mind if I keep mine on, do you? I'm a nature gal and all, but I'm not quite ready for that level of nature. Ya know, snakes and such."

A laugh bubbled up as I saw the sheepish grin on her face. "Snakes? Not much to worry about if you pay attention." I rubbed the back of my leg and the still tingling skin around the fang marks. The whole leg itched like crazy underneath the stiff denim. She rolled her eyes and snorted.

Faint rumblings had her gazing at the sky, then at me. I shrugged. The impending storm was written all over the trees. Their leaves were turning upside down, a sure sign of coming rain. The air was filled with heavy, damp smells.

"Hmm. I remember seeing these when I was here last time," she mused, running her fingers over a tiny carving in one trunk as we passed by. "I wondered who made them."

I took her hand and placed a finger in each of the divots that fell inside the circle.

"Me, Mom, Jack, the old man, Biscuit," I murmured, tracing the outer edge.

Jessica tilted her head, capturing my gaze, an odd mix of emotions flitting across her face. Every time we came to a tree that I had marked, she took a moment to touch the circle.

We approached the crash site, breaking the tree line and standing side by side in the overgrown grass. It was wilder than it had been the year Jessica had camped there, saplings springing up all around as the forest continued its relentless reclamation. Birds wheeled and sang overhead, disturbed by us traipsing through their kingdom. Small creatures scattered at the sound of our footsteps over the rough terrain, their frenzied flights sounding more like bears crashing through the forest than the pint-sized madness of startled squirrels and chipmunks.

When we stepped into the central dip of where the plane had crashed, Jessica turned to me. "Do you know what happened, Lily? Why the plane went down in the first place?"

I stared at her, baffled by the fact that I had never once considered there had been a reason we'd plunged from the sky. In all my years on this wild mountain, I had never questioned anything other than what to do for my own survival. I'd never asked Jack, I'd never asked the old man, and it had never crossed my mind that it was something other than chance that had left me stranded in these mountains.

"According to what the NTSB said, there was an explosion, a crack in the fuselage or something like that near the front of the plane. It ripped the cockpit clean off and sent the tail end, where you were, flying straight over this mountain. They didn't know it at the time, really. They went looking for the black box and found that about twenty miles over in the next valley. It took them a week to trace the debris back to the bigger pieces of the cockpit. They searched everywhere for the tail but couldn't find anything."

I didn't understand half of what she said but got the gist of it all, nodding. "It blew up. There was a storm, and when I got back here, it was gone." I put my arms up, gesturing to the huge dead trees that lined the clearing. "Well, not gone, just…

everywhere. I didn't know what to do, so I went back to the cave."

I took her hand and guided her to one of the thick dead trees that surrounded the crash site, putting her fingers over the shrapnel that peppered deep into the peeling char. Her eyes widened as she felt the metal edges. She explored a few other trees, shaking her head as she mumbled about the force it would have taken to make those shards disappear into the trunks.

"I bet it looked like a meteor strike under the canopy here. That explains why nobody ever found it. All the reports said there were torrential rains around that time that held up a lot of the searching. They never expected to find any survivors, and recovery wasn't a pressing issue. I guess they're going to be kicking themselves on that one," she muttered wryly. "Two survivors, then one. You grew up out here, and no one ever had a clue you even existed. When I came up a few years back, there was a lot of gossip, you know. Locals always have their stories—the Ozark Howler, the Gowrow, the Fouke Monster, all the usual suspects—but out here, I heard a few campers talking about 'the Woodsman.' They said he would mess with their food stores and chase them out of the forest. That was you, wasn't it?"

I shrugged, causing her to break into a smile for the first time since we had entered the clearing. It lit up her face and caused a shiver to race down my spine. Something about her manner, her voice, her presence seemed to be slowly undoing me. Jessica continued to walk around, using her hiking boots to overturn rocks as she went.

"What are you looking for?"

"I don't know, really. I guess just some sign that he was here, that he still is." She turned away, lost once more in sorrow.

I knew what she needed, and I wasn't sure if I had anything that would help, but I figured it was worth a shot. I pointed to the other side of clearing in the direction of my waterfall, wanting to lead her to where I had spent the last eight years. Over time, most of the clothing had been worn beyond repair, and the useless items of my collection had been left to rot in the damp air. There were still little things, trinkets and buttons and other stuff I didn't understand, metals and plastics that would last for hundreds of years if left undisturbed. My need to share my secrets with her was powerful and overwhelming. She followed as I walked.

I traced the route I had walked innumerable times over the years, not a game trail but a path left by my own two feet wearing a streak of naked dirt between the twisting trees. I could feel the heaviness of her gaze and the soft fluttering of her emotions tickling my exposed skin. We were matched well in all the words we could not speak, and for the first time, I felt like there was someone who had the same sort of hidden world within her as I did. Her silence was oddly comforting.

As we approached the waterfall, I waited for her to take in the beauty of our surroundings. I could see her confusion when I stopped at the pool, sitting on a rock to dip my toes into the still cold water. She took her time sizing up the area, checking out the stone circle of my firepit, the wildflowers that rioted along the tree line, the animal prints of every size leading in and out of the brush.

I gazed into the darkening sky and saw that the storm was nearly upon us. "We should go in. It's going to start raining soon."

"In where?"

I gestured toward the falls, taking immense pleasure from her quizzical expression. I hopped across the rocks and slipped into the opening of the cave, hearing a peal of laughter as she realized there was an opening behind the thin sheets of water. She stepped into my cave a moment after me, awe painted across her face as she took in the large room. When I slipped through the practically invisible crevasse, I heard her call my name. I stopped and reached back, waving for her to follow.

"Damn, that's a tight fit," Jessica mumbled as she bumped into me when she popped into the cavern I called home. I felt her reaching for the flashlight around her belt, and I put out a hand to stop her.

"You don't need that." I knelt next to the fire ring and set about lighting the tinder kept in a pile close by my kindling. In a few moments, we had a small glow of fire, then a fine little blaze that lit the room warmly.

She gasped when the light grew, hand over her mouth as she looked from the rock ledges filled with my things to the walls decorated with artwork, both new and ancient. "Are you freaking kidding me? What is this place? It's like stepping back in time ten thousand years."

She wandered around, drawing lightly along each new surface in the same way I had at the hotel. She stretched to reach some of the older paintings, then brushed across the crude, chalky drawings I had done over the years. I dragged a suitcase to the fire and opened it, revealing years' worth of journaling done in pen, pencil, then finally a mixture of ash and clay that I had used with sharpened sticks. She sifted through it carefully, reading snippets here and there and occasionally shaking her head.

"In my head, I knew you were telling the truth, but…this is *surreal*. You were here all this time, all alone."

Her voice quivered as she spoke, and I felt compelled to tell her that I had not always been alone. In a quiet tone, I told her of the old man, his dog, and our unlikely alliance. I spoke of the lessons he'd taught me before the sickness had taken him and the loyalty of my canine companion as we'd both grieved.

"The skull was Biscuit's? I'm sorry. I had no idea what I was looking at. I just knew that skull was buried long after the plane crash, and I thought if I could figure out who did it, maybe I could find out exactly what happened. When I woke up and found it reburied in the same spot, it sure spooked me. I thought long and hard about just how haunted these woods were. I've thought about that day for so long. If I had known you were there, maybe I could have—"

"I wasn't ready to be found. You walked right past me, close enough I could have reached out and touched you."

"That's a bit creepy, although I should have figured it out. It felt like someone was just out of reach, playing with me. I shook it off because I thought I was being overly dramatic. I always get a little nervous camping alone, but... The second night, when I tossed a few sticks into the fire, I could have sworn I saw someone standing a few feet away. Guess my instincts were right on. When I downloaded the footage from the trail cams, I could not believe what I saw. Honestly, I thought someone was screwing with me." She wrinkled her nose and shivered. "Geez. Even after I saw those footprints when the skull disappeared, I was convinced I was hallucinating. I see it now, though, after walking with you. You're like a ghost out here. Of course, that doesn't excuse you from being a total creeper and scaring the bejeezus out of me."

The enormity of that statement struck me like a meteor to the solar plexus. I *was* a ghost for all those years, invisible, dead in the eyes of the world, merely haunting the forest. I scrunched my brows as I contemplated her comment, finally realizing she was teasing me. Our eyes caught and held; the awkwardness and strain began to fall away as I grinned back.

"Well, you've lived one of the most fascinating stories I've ever heard. Keep going."

The cave reverberated with a crack of lightning, making Jessica flinch and scoot closer to the fire. I squeezed my lips together to keep from laughing as she shivered again. The glittering of her eyes in the firelight gave me pause, sending a wholly different shiver down my spine, one that stole my breath with its force. I felt as though I could not get enough of her, wanting to creep across the floor and press myself along the length of her body. I did not understand the depth and breadth of these new feelings or even what they meant, yet they echoed through my blood and bones, drumming deep within my soul.

Composing myself, I told her all about my forays in the woods, my encounters with the local wildlife, my gentle terrorizing of the campers. She laughed outright when I told her how I had once stolen all the pants off a makeshift clothesline and watched the confused, half-dressed campers gathering what was left of their belongings in their underwear. Between my stories stretched great lengths of contemplation for both of us, companionable silences that left us staring mesmerized into the crackling flames.

After one of these epic pauses, Jessica tilted her head and frowned slightly. "What was your mother like? I can't imagine she was anything like that crusty curmudgeon at the hospital."

"No, nothing like that. She was…I can't really remember her very good."

"Me, neither. My dad was awesome, and I remember how much I loved him, but the little things are eaten away by time. I'm just left with the feeling of him. It's awful to think that even his picture seems unfamiliar now." She dropped her head into her hands.

"It doesn't matter what he looked like. It matters that he

loved you, and you loved him. Like Biscuit. He didn't care
what I looked like, only that I was good to him. He didn't have
to have eyes to know that I loved him, only a heart."

"You know, in all my years, I never thought my life would
lead me here to you. I loved fairy tales as a child, the wilder
the better, and my dad would always tell me these whoppers
that were off the charts *crazy*. Sitting here with you is almost
like this was his last gift for me, a real fairy tale. Not that what
you lived has been this wonderful existence, but you know
what I mean."

"It's okay here, quiet and safe. I never have to worry about
much. It *was* nice to use a real toilet again, though," I mused,
pulling another giggle from Jessica. "And hot water. That stuff
is great, but I'm pretty sure I could live without airplanes."

She snorted at the last remark as if trying hard not to
laugh. It was exhilarating listening to the sounds of her joy
that tickled the center of my being, warming me. "Airplanes
aren't that bad as long as they do what's asked of them. I fly
all the time for stories. I'm a freelance journalist." I looked
at her blankly, hoping she would explain. "I write articles
for magazines and newspapers. I cover the kind of things my
father would have loved: supposed miracles, claims of alien
abductions, cryptids, and crazies. Ironic, huh?"

"What's a cryptid?"

"Creatures that scientists don't think are real. Usually,
there are myths and legends passed down about them in
different cultures or regions. I go into it with a healthy dose of
skepticism, but there are a ton of unexplained phenomena that
occur all over the world, all the time. Sometimes, we find the
answers, but sometimes, we don't. Never know if you don't
look, though."

I was lost in the cadence of her voice, content to bask in
the curve of her smile. She flipped through the pages I had

written again, picking out a few to read fully, digesting them with a faraway look on her face.

"I ran out of paper a while ago."

I remember the helpless feeling of not having anything else to write on, the sadness of losing that last connection with my mother. Ink hadn't been an issue. I just watered down clay and ashes from the fire and dipped the tip of my pen in the slurry.

"What is this?" She pointed to a crude drawing on one of the sheets.

"That's Henry, the mountain lion. He, I mean, *she*, lives here, too."

"In this cave?" Jessica looked around as if startled at the prospect.

I let out a bark of laughter, startling her further. "No. She lives in the woods. She just comes here to get a drink. Sometimes, she brings babies with her, but I haven't seen them in a long time. I used to take meat from her when I didn't have any. I quit because I didn't want to take it from her when she has babies to feed."

"Befriended a mountain lion, huh? That's pretty cool. How come her name is Henry?"

"She isn't really my friend. I'm pretty sure she would eat me if she got the chance. For a long time, I thought she was a boy because I never got very close to her, but then I saw her babies."

"I can't even begin to fathom the life you've lived. You aren't even twenty, and you've had more catastrophe, more calamity, than any person I've ever met, yet here you are, still smiling in spite of it all." She stared at me over the flames, shaking her head once more. "Quite the enigma, aren't you?"

❖

We sat like that for a long time, waiting out the flashing and banging of the spring storm. There were words between us stacked like bricks that we could neither speak nor remove. All the joviality from earlier had leaked from the room, leaving an echo chamber of regret that stretched far into the ether. Thin tendrils of smoke curled skyward, escaping through the invisible crack in the ceiling, and the flames sent shadows dancing around us like spirits. We munched granola bars and pondered our separateness together. It must have been a half hour, maybe longer, before she spoke again.

"Lily? I have a question for you, and I don't want you to answer right away. I want you to think about it for a while, really mull it over. Would you let me write your story? Not some short, edited version for a crappy rag, but the whole thing. Straight from your mouth." I made to reply, and she stopped me with a raised hand. "You need to think about it because there are going to be a lot of other people who will want to do it. They are going to offer you more money than you could ever spend, and all I can offer is the promise that your story will be the truest version I can muster. I'm not sure I can do it the justice it deserves, and there are loads of people who could write circles around me, but I think my dad would have wanted me to try."

"You want to write about me? A book?" When she nodded, I scurried over to another case where I had the two novels I had found among the belongings in the plane. "Like these?" I sat next to her and held the well-worn paperbacks out. I hesitated a moment, blushing when I realized that the pages in certain areas were dogeared and tattered. Those were the parts I'd read voraciously by the firelight, ashamed of the thrill the dirty language gave me as I imagined each scene.

"Interesting choice in literature." She flipped them over and read the backs.

"I…I found them."

"Nora Roberts and H. P. Lovecraft, huh? You read them both?"

"Yeah. I only read that one once. It was too scary."

"H. P. Lovecraft was a master at horror. I can't imagine how terrifying it would be to read his stories for the first time all alone in the woods. Hell, I can barely read some of it now without having nightmares. Excellent writer, though. Nora Roberts, too. She can really write the pants off a romance novel, pardon the pun." Jessica giggled at her own joke as I fought back the heat of embarrassment. "At least you got the best of both worlds as far as authors go. What other stuff do you have?"

I pointed to the stack of manuals on a far ledge. They were in terrible condition, damp, with the pages glued together in many spots. I also grabbed the little bird book I had ruined when I fell into the water. "This was mine."

After she looked over the manuals for a moment, she held the pocket guide in her hands gently. "Seen better days, huh?"

"I wasn't careful enough. I fell in the water."

"Happens to the best of us, my dear. I've dropped probably a dozen books in the bathtub, including one very expensive anatomy and physiology textbook two days before my final exam. Books can be replaced, though, right? Was it a bad fall?"

I thought back to the moment I'd opened my eyes and seen the old man's panicked face hovering over me. I still had a scar on my shoulder and the sharp edge of my front tooth to remind me. "I didn't die, so not that bad, I guess."

"Hmm." She was staring at me intently, tilting her head as I squirmed under the scrutiny. "Well, to answer your question, no. I can't write nearly as good as those two can, but it'll probably be a lot more palatable than the manuals and not quite so dry as the bird book." She touched each of the books once more before setting them down.

"I don't mind if you want to write about me."

"No, no. You should probably talk to your grandmother about it or a lawyer or something. You can't just say yes, or I'll feel like I'm taking advantage of you because you're...I..."

I couldn't tell whether I should be insulted by her comment or not, so instead, I chose to ignore it. "Let's go look at the water. It's really pretty when it rains."

She followed me through the crevasse and to the entrance, where the falls were thick and muddy, the strong water flowing heavily and the pool below a good foot higher then when we had arrived. "We won't get stuck in here, will we?"

"No, it goes down quick. The rain stopped a while ago. It won't take long for the water to lighten up. The first storm was the worst, when I found this place. The water was almost to the floor there, and it lasted *forever*. That was when I had Jack's watch, though, and everything seemed slower when I could see what time it was. The compass helped me find my way in the woods. After a while, when I figured out which direction was which, I didn't need it much. I guess that was good because I broke it when I ruined my bird book."

"My mom and I bought it for his birthday that year. When his old one died, we had a heck of a time finding one with all the faces on it like he liked. We went to five different jewelers before we found it. I'm...I'm glad it helped you."

I ducked my head, ashamed that my own clumsy actions had killed her father's watch. "Tell me more about your mother."

"I dunno what to say. She's a great mom, fun and caring. It took a lot out of her when my dad didn't come home, and then two of my aunts came to stay with us for a few months. She bounced back after a while, though, and ended up marrying my uncle's best friend. His name is Francis. They're divorced now, but I still hang out with him every few weeks to catch up. He is a good guy, a mechanic."

"Does she wear dresses? My mom always wore dresses."

"Not really. Mostly, she's in scrubs. She's a nurse."

"Oh. Like Abigail?"

"Yup, just like her. She doesn't much appreciate my obsession with the plane crash and all that. She was pissed when I came up here the summer they discovered where the tail went down. No, pissed is the wrong word. She was... heartbroken. She felt it all over again when they called and told her dad's wallet had been found by some campers. I offered to come down and check it out when the local PD said it was intact. I mean, how does a wallet survive a plane crash *and* an explosion, then find its way to civilization years later? It didn't make any sense. I had no idea what I would be walking into when I saw you. The hospital almost didn't let me talk to you at first. They were concerned about your 'fragile state' and all. The squeaky wheel gets the grease, though, and by the second day, I think they realized it was either let me talk to you or haul me out in handcuffs."

"I was surprised to see you."

"The feeling was mutual. When I saw your hair, I knew you were the one from the trail cam picture. My dad couldn't have talked about me that much. How did you even remember who I was?"

"He had your picture in his wallet, and he talked about you a lot. You still keep your hair braided like the picture. Jack told me what a good soccer player you are and how you won lots of ribbons in horse shows."

"A long time ago, yeah. I mean, I still ride horses, but I'm not into showing anymore. I've got a nice little half-Arab mare I used to compete on. She's retired now, so we hack out every once in a while, just to keep the juices flowing. I haven't played soccer in forever."

"I've never ridden a horse."

"Oh, we can fix that. I saw a rental outfit about an hour north of the campsite. I'll take you out there one of these days and see if we can get a guided trail ride or something."

"Really?"

"Hell, yeah. I'm always busting at the seams to get back in the saddle, so why not? It's gotten awfully dark, and the water still looks rough. I guess we're camping here tonight." She raised an eyebrow at me and screwed up her lips. "You turkey. You did that on purpose, didn't you?"

I wandered away, feigning innocence as my internal voice shrieked with happiness at the thought of being home for the night. My bladder, however, was less than impressed with the lack of plumbing. A short time in civilization and here I was, spoiled by a few pipes and some porcelain, pining for a stream of scalding water to run over my chilly skin. I could hear echoes of the old man's voice in my head, muttering that I had gone soft already. Soon, it was Jessica's voice grumbling playfully about the same issues I was lamenting as she slipped through the crevasse. I sat watching the back of the falls for a while before joining her at the fire for a few pieces of fruit to sustain us through the night.

"Did you recognize me when I was up here camping?"

"Yes, kind of. I knew I *should* have known who you were. You looked so familiar, but I didn't know why until I saw you at the hospital."

"You looked at me like I had come to rescue you, you know. It was terrifying."

"I'm sorry."

"Don't be. I'm glad you did. It made me believe you."

Firelight blazed in the dark chamber, cracking and popping

companionably while I dragged a few ragged blankets near the warmth. It sent a flickering glow over Jessica as she fed it, the flames licking gently along the fresh wood in its limitless hunger.

I stripped to my bone necklace, intending to stretch out on the soft cloth, but her eyes stopped me, pinning me fast as she stared over the dancing fire. When she finally averted her gaze, I sank gratefully to the blanket, goose bumps pebbling my exposed skin. I peeked through the slits of my eyelids, curiosity peeling away the layers of modesty that warned me to look away as she undressed. Her body was a wonder, different, a dark side to my light, thick with muscles in a way I was lacking. Her thighs and calves were sharply defined, her shoulders broader, the swell of her breasts heavier than mine. There was beauty in the economy of movement as she shed her outer layers down to her shorts and a tank top, unlike the gangly and awkward way I tripped out of the loose jeans. I wondered if I would ever have the kind of self-possession she embodied in those scant moments of undress.

"Were you lonely? Up here, I mean." She was staring at the ceiling as she asked, lying back on the blanket I had laid out for her. It was cleaner than the rest, but I still caught sight of her wrinkling her nose at the smell.

"Sometimes. Sometimes not."

"What did you think about at night?"

"The stars, mostly. How they moved. What it would be like to see them up close. How small I was compared to the trees. Some nights, I felt like the only person on Earth."

"Were you ever scared?"

"No. Not scared. Well, I was for a while after Biscuit left, but once I got used to it, it was kind of nice. I don't know how to describe it."

"I understand, I think. Camping is kinda therapeutic for

me. A way to lose myself to nature. My dad and I used to go all the time so now, the woods remind me of him." Her dark eyes glittered in the firelight as she stared across the flames at me. "Most people would go crazy being on their own for that long, though. Why didn't you try to get help after the plane went down?"

"I don't know. I didn't belong, I guess. I never really fit in anywhere. Not school, not sports, not anywhere. The only person who made me feel happy was my mother and…I fit in here, though. No one looks at me funny or talks about how weird I am. All the birds and rabbits and squirrels just keep going, like sharing their home with me is no big deal." I looked away, convinced she would think I was just plain crazy. "I'm sorry."

"For what?"

"For being weird."

"I don't think you're weird, Lily. Sometimes, we just need to find a place to be ourselves. If this is your place, I can totally understand that. It's beautiful here. Peaceful. It breaks my heart to know that you thought this was the only place you could be you, though. You don't have to apologize for feeling that way. I, for one, feel like that pretty often, and I bet lots of other people do, too."

"You don't fit in?"

"Not really. Half the time, I don't even know who I am, let alone where I belong."

"But you're…"

"Normal? What's normal, anyway? Normal is overrated."

We were both quiet for a while, staring at the shadows playing across the stone and dirt. I could feel her eyes flit over to me occasionally, working through the messiness of my mind, finding her own answers to questions I could not hear.

Sleep overtook us when the silence stretched further, a deep and dreamless chunk of time passed in the blink of an eye.

❖

I crept out of the cave when dawn broke, surprised to see tracks on the muddy bank. Henry had come while we'd slept, kittens at foot. The tracks played around the pool in a flurry of activity, mingling with deer, possum, and raccoon prints. The water was lower, nearly normal, yet still the color of chocolate milk, and the sun rose to a warm, cloudless sky as it drew steam from the damp ground like a ghostly mist where it penetrated the trees. It smelled of wood rot, leaf litter, and earthworms, the scent wrapping me in a blanket of happiness. Late spring was the most beautiful season here, filled with the sickly sweet scent of flowers and a chorus of wildlife finding their new rhythm in the growing daylight. By the time summer rolled around, it would be quieter during the day, but there would come a raucous opera that would start as soon as the night took hold.

I was sobered by the thought that I might not see summer on my mountain again. The sights and sounds, the scents, the freedom were sand through my fingertips, caught on the breeze and drifting away. As I watched the brilliant sun crest the treetops, I did not look away, determined to burn this lovely memory into my brain in the hope that it would last forever. I was torn. The overwhelming urge to hide in the forest and wish away events of the past few days pulled at me strongly, but there was another feeling, a longing hidden deep down that I couldn't quite pinpoint.

The crack of a twig drew my gaze to the sleep-tousled Jessica approaching. Her dark hair hung loose and wild as she blinked in the morning sun. My heart seized at the sight, the simpleness of my newfound feelings for her nearly frothing out of my cracking chest. It was stronger than anything I had ever felt and far more terrifying.

Jessica stretched and sat on the rock to my left, draping a casual arm across my shoulders as she shielded her eyes with her other hand. I was stiff and out of sorts, afraid any move might give away what I had just been thinking. The easy manner with which she leaned into me, warm against the morning chill, slowly chipped away at the wall that was holding me together.

"You would think that under all these trees, you'd never get to see the sun rise, but man alive, this is something else." She tipped her head back and sighed, staring up at the brightening sky. "Thank you for sharing this with me."

"You're not mad?"

"Why would I be mad?"

"'Cause of the rain and staying here all night."

She laughed softly. "I think I needed this, too. It makes me feel a little closer to my dad. I had a dream about him last night. Most of it is pretty fuzzy in my mind, but he was fishing in the pond near our house while I watched from the kitchen window. He pulled you out of the water and laid you on the ground, then he turned and waved to me. Before I could run outside, he walked off into the pond. I watched him disappear, and there was nothing I could do." She brushed away a few tears. "I guess that's as good a good-bye as I'll ever get, huh?"

I didn't know how to respond, so I closed my eyes. Jack was as much a part of these mountains as I was. Did she feel him here the way that I did? Could she feel the rest of them, too? I could. Would I still feel them if I left?

When the sky had fully broken with daylight, we rose and returned to the cave for the final time to bid farewell to my home. I stuffed my journals and the two books into my backpack, choosing to leave just about everything else behind. I cleaned out the ash from the stone circle and left one final mark on the cave wall, pressing Jessica's handprint next to mine at the entrance. I took the old man's gnarled walking stick, swiped from his front porch after I had found his body, the worn handhold a small comfort in the face of all that was happening. Other than those few small things, I needed nothing of this past life. It occurred to me that by leaving it all behind, I was allowing myself to choose a different future or perhaps allowing for a different future to choose me. The pack sagged and cut into my shoulder with the weight of its burden, yet the pain was no match to the agony unfurling inside me.

We hiked in silence to the car, a pair of strangers once more, sharing a sun dappled path in a wild forest. I led slowly, not because of the heavy pack but because of the weight of my sorrow. My bare feet led me toward the unknown, away from the safety of my solitude. I felt a deep and abiding kinship with these mountains, already aware of the pea-sized hollow spot inside me growing exponentially with every step. By the time my toes hit the gravel edge of the parking lot, I nearly crumpled to the ground. Jessica gathered me close, catching my tears with her shoulder as I sobbed.

CHAPTER EIGHT

The ride to the hotel seemed brief compared to how long it had taken to get to the mountains. A headache pulsed its way up from my core, clinging and rattling along the frazzled nerves that held me together like loose twine. It felt as though parts of my body could just drop off at any time, never to be seen again. I imagined leaving a trail of my pieces from the mountain to the hotel, human breadcrumbs to help me find my way back. I would gather them as I returned, making myself whole again by the time I reached the wood's edge. What was it that I was giving up, and what was I receiving in exchange? Thoughts like these climbed the folds of my brain, looking for a crack to escape through. The answers were impossible to conceive.

The closer we got to the hotel, the more Jessica's phone rang. When she had first turned it on, it dinged and whistled, and the sounds continued as the miles slipped beneath the tires. She occasionally glanced at the screen but never answered. Every time the melody would sound, her lips would get thinner and thinner, pursed with disgust.

"This isn't good." We drove past the hotel, and the parking lot was filled to the brim with utter chaos. "Do you still have Abigail's number?"

"Uh-huh." I dug the folded paper out of my pocket. Jessica tossed me her phone.

"Call her. There's no way we can go back there." I stared at the black rectangle that rested lightly in my palms, trying not to look as confused as I felt. There were no buttons, no lights, just a smooth dark screen. I don't know if it was my perplexed expression or the fact that I did nothing but stare at the phone, but she soon pulled off to the side of the road.

"Sorry, I forget you've been living under a literal rock for the last decade. Here, let me show you how this works. I'll put it on speaker so we can both hear." She explained the phone, letting me tap in the numbers and make the call.

Abigail picked up on the first ring. "Hello?" Her voice sounded clear and strong, as though she was sitting in the car with us.

"Hello?" I replied, unsure what to say beyond that single word.

"Lily, is that you? Honey, are you okay? I saw the circus found out where you were staying. It's all over the news, and they've got people camping out everywhere. I even saw one station sent their people out into the woods to find you, but those sad sacks got lost and had to get park rangers in to drag them out in the pouring rain. Buncha fools, if you ask me." Abigail's tone of exasperation was clear as she spoke.

"Abby, we need a place to crash or something until this dies down. Anything you can suggest?" Jessica leaned over, brushing my arm as she spoke.

"Sure, but you aren't going to like it."

"Ugh. Look, I know it sounds like a lot to ask, but can't we just hide out at your place for a day or two? I don't know that either one of us is ready to leave just yet."

"I live with my daughter and my grandbabies. We don't even have enough room to invite a flea over, let alone you two and the rest of America. Lily's grandmother has security out the wazoo at her place, according to what she told me. Other than trying to get the police to put you in protective custody, I don't think you're gonna find a safer spot right now. Besides, if you don't take her there, Granny's liable to get the whole world out looking for her 'kidnapped' granddaughter." Jessica groaned. "If I were you, I'd definitely be booking it across the state line before people get wind that you aren't holed up in your room. The sooner, the better. I'll text you the address. I'm not saying it's the only place, but I think, odds are, you've got no other decent options. Her picture is pasted all over the TV as we speak."

I could barely process the conversation. Everything in me wanted to flee back to the safety of my cave, away from the madness of civilization. All this talk of state lines and security had my head whirling with fear. "Dumb snake," I whispered under my breath. "Dumb me." It was all my fault.

"Shit." Jessica caught my eye and sighed. "Fine. Send me the address, and we'll head out now."

"Be careful. I'll call the old bat and let her know you're on your way," Abigail said, laughing as she hung up.

We spent a long minute in the close confines of the Subaru on the side of the highway, breathing in one another's air, letting the tension walk a tightrope between us, listening to the rumbling of passing cars. I squirmed uncomfortably, wishing more than anything to be away from all the chaos.

I heard Jessica sigh again, looked up to find her eyes boring into mine. She reached across the console and took my hand, giving it a gentle squeeze that spoke volumes. Her irises remained unfathomably dark despite the sunlight streaming into them. I could feel my color rising as she studied me, wondering what could possibly hold her interest so intently.

"I find myself willing to do unthinkable things to make

sure you're safe. Why is that?" A wry smile curved at the edges of her mouth, crinkling up the skin next to her eyes as she turned forward and eased the car back onto the asphalt. "This is not going to end well for me. Not well at all, and I'm too stupid to walk away."

I had no idea how to respond, feeling that she did not need me to step into the conversation she was having with herself. Her tone was light, soothing, nothing that matched her words at all. I felt myself stretching thinner and thinner with every mile that passed.

The drive took hours longer than it should have because I did not travel well. The car brought back memories of my childhood, journeying from one rest stop to the next so I could relieve my rioting stomach. Jessica was more patient than I deserved, once even rubbing my back as I gagged in the tall grass on the side of the road. The touch of her hand sent shivers along my spine, making me forget all about the heaving and rolling of my insides.

After what seemed like an eternity of driving, she began to drum her fingers on the steering wheel, her trimmed nails tapping out a ghost of a tune that rattled around in my head. What was it? I had heard it before, a long time ago. When her humming got a little softer, it finally occurred to me; that was the same tune Jack had hummed. I turned toward the window to hide my tears.

The air began to smell salty, and the vegetation changed considerably. I watched the sea coming into focus in the distance, sand swirling in the breeze, gulls cavorting overhead, wheeling and diving at one another.

"That's a *pelican*," I exclaimed, startling Jessica out of her thoughts.

She leaned forward and glanced up as the huge bird glided

across the road. "A big one. Probably off to go fishing for his dinner."

"There weren't any pelicans near the big river, but there were lots of other birds. There were gray ones, herons, with great big wingspans and little ruby-throated hummingbirds that sounded like bees. Woodpeckers. There were lots of different woodpeckers in the trees. The red-bellies are my favorite. They have bright red heads and black and white backs, but their bellies aren't really red at all. They are kind of light pink. We had them in Pennsylvania, too, in our backyard."

Jessica listened without comment, flicking her eyes over to me as I spoke, then right back to the busy road. I chattered on, nervousness giving my voice a slight tremor, but I could not seem to turn off the faucet of my thoughts. While she observed me with curiosity, she did not interrupt the steady stream of my speech. I spoke more in the last ten minutes of our drive than I had in the last ten years.

She turned down a less-traveled road, aiming toward the sea that had disappeared behind the built-up suburbs. Within five minutes, we turned again and stopped at a huge gate. Jessica gave my grandmother's information to the guard, and we waited for him to press the appropriate buttons. Soon enough, we were cruising through gates, driving down an empty street between houses that towered over their pristine landscaping and sandy surroundings. Each one had a long and curving driveway of colorful paving stones and large amounts of empty acreage. Palm trees lined the road, not a frond out of place. The driveway we entered was as imposing as the rest, leading to a monstrous house with a set of cement steps to the front door. An older, gray-haired woman waited to guide us to the back of the house to park.

When we rounded the house, there was a huge expanse

of sand that led all the way to the waters of the Gulf, bringing back memories I could hardly grasp. The smells that met me reminded me of gathering seashells and sand dollars with my mother. The feeling was intense, and I didn't wait for the car to stop completely before I leapt out, sprinting across the dunes. If Jessica called after me, it was lost in the rush of air as I flew along the warm white sand. The only thing that stopped my forward motion was the water, slipping in and out, leaving the sucking wet sand that I dug my toes into with pleasure.

"Christ almighty, you run like a freaking gazelle," Jessica puffed out as she stopped, winded and red, beside me with her hands pressing her sides.

I pointed to the tiny triangles of white dotting the horizon. "Look at all the boats out there."

"Sailboats, probably out sport fishing. Perfect season for hooking mahi-mahi and sailfish." Her breathing slowed as we watched them drift along the water. She leaned down and picked up a little white shard poking up from the sand, turning it over in the thin layer of water. "Shark tooth." She handed it to me. I pulled my necklace out and held the shark tooth next to it, marveling at the differences as the water played along the tips of my toes, advancing and retreating like a shy puppy.

"I bet we could find a few more and make you a whole necklace. Those are bear teeth, right? I'm half afraid to ask how many bears you had to wrestle to get all those."

"I wrestled as many bears to get these teeth as you wrestled sharks to get this one." I laughed long and hard at the thought of the two of us going toe to toe with the huge predators just to steal their teeth.

She made a muscle and wiggled her eyebrows. "How do you know I'm not a professional shark wrestler? I might have a megalodon stuffed and hanging over my mantel!"

We both dissolved into giggles, stumbling backward

and collapsing in the dry dunes as we gasped for breath. We passed the tooth back and forth, holding it up, rubbing the smooth sides and serrated edges. Our reverie was cut short by a shadow: Dawn, umbrella in hand, frowning at our upturned faces.

"Not exactly the hello I had expected."

Jessica scrambled to her feet like a naughty child while I gazed at both of them, one face severe and unyielding, the other glinting with repressed mischief. I grinned, having no intention of rising. If I could not return to the forest, I would be content to float on a bed of sand and sea until the end of my days, a beach creature taken by the tide, at the mercy of the moon. I closed my eyes and let the sound of the water, the shriek of gulls, and the rustling of the breeze through the tanglehead and cordgrass fill me up till I felt ready to burst. The two women standing over me walked off, immersed in a conversation I did not care to hear.

❖

I lay on the beach for hours, frittering away the afternoon running my fingers through the sand, looking for more shark teeth, and playing with the tiny mussels that spit and bubbled as they burrowed. Jessica came for me as the sun was dipping low in the western sky and led me up the dunes to a little cottage off the back of the main house. There was a washroom right off the entryway, and she sent me in to bathe the day from my well-baked skin. I let the piping hot water envelop me, reveling in the smells of all the bottles standing like soldiers on the white ledge of the shower. When I felt sufficiently clean, I wrapped myself in a fluffy white towel and went to find Jessica.

She waited in an enclosed sunroom, back to the door,

staring out over the Gulf with her arms crossed. Her dark hair, braided and still slightly damp from her own shower, hung long against her, leaving wet marks on the back of her shirt. She looked up at my reflection in the glass and turned. My heart tripped, somersaulting in my chest as our eyes locked. Suddenly, the scenes from the book I had read on the mountain came rushing back to me. I could feel the blush starting in my cheeks and whooshing all the way to my toes. My stomach popped and fizzed like I had swallowed fireworks.

Whatever my body was screaming at me, it would not be ignored any longer. Her eyes burned into mine, unreadable and intense, skewering me to the spot and stealing what little voice I might have mustered. There was something different in her stance, a hardness, an iron resolve, as though she had made up her mind about an important matter I hadn't known existed.

Dawn was perched on the loveseat a few feet away. "Jessica has informed me you would find this cottage more comfortable than the main house. I've had your things brought in and set up. There are clothes laid out for you on the bed in the first room. While you will be afforded a significant amount of autonomy, you will take your meals with me. There is an intercom system connecting both houses, and should you have any issues or needs, press the button to speak to the head housekeeper, Mrs. Mackle." She stopped and looked at her watch, tapping the face. "We're already late to dinner. Please get dressed. I'll wait here and show you the way."

Was this what life was to become for me? Barked orders and meals by the clock? I could feel my anger rising and the grit of my teeth against one another as I clenched my jaw. I wanted to scream and pound my fist on the floor like I'd done when I was little. I waited a heartbeat, then two, then three, counting away the worst of my anger until I could feel my muscles relaxing.

When I didn't retreat to follow her direction, Jessica walked over and led me down the hall to the bedroom, shutting the door behind us. She sat on the bed heavily and dropped her head into her hands. For a moment, I thought she was crying, but instead, when she looked up, her face was the picture of calm.

"I'm sorry I brought you here. I knew it would be like this, but I didn't think we had any other options. She'll take good care of you. Don't let her badger you into changing who you are, Lily. She isn't your keeper. I'll leave my number here. Call if you need me or just want to talk."

"What do you mean? Are you leaving?"

"I've been formally invited to skip town, do not pass go, do not collect two hundred dollars. Granny Dawn feels I'd be an inappropriate role model for her young, impressionable, sheltered granddaughter."

"Why?"

"It's hard to explain, Lily."

"You can't go. I need you here. What will I do without you?"

"That's exactly why I need to go."

"But—"

She cut me off before I could tell her how important she was to me. "Lily, stop. I can't be around you right now. Things are…confusing, and I don't want to make a horrible mistake. I'll call you when I get home." She stood abruptly, closing the distance between us and crushing me in a tight hug. "This isn't forever, you know. Just for now."

It was an eerie echo of what I had told myself as I'd drawn a cover over my mother in the plane. Just for now. Just for now was just a fancy way of saying *the end* without having to use those words. Lying to myself about it had only prolonged the agony, and I feared the results would be the same this time, as well.

As her arms released me, I felt my heart drop. This was Jack's daughter, the girl I had "known" most of my life through the memory of his stories and that one, worn picture. She was leaving, just like he had, barely a stone's throw from our meeting. Was I destined to lose everyone I loved? The air left the room with her, opening a great sucking hole that mirrored the one left by Biscuit, only this one felt deeper, emptier, chewing at my aching insides.

❖

I dressed without noticing the stylish cuts and colors of the expensive clothes, leaving the impossible-to-maneuver bra on the floor in a fit of disgust. Dawn walked with me along the short path to the main house and guided me into the dining room. The house was huge, with high ceilings and wood floors. Everything was clean and gleaming, even the banister of the curling staircase. The table, though long and dark, was set with sprays of fresh-cut flowers and a lacy white runner. The solid chairs stood tall and imposing, uncomfortably hard against my spine as I slouched forward.

"Sit up, child. There is no place at this table for lazy posture."

I glared at her across the dark expanse, hating everything from the sound of her voice to the stiff shoulders that jutted out in a perfect, unmovable-looking T.

"I understand this is a difficult change for you, but I am not your enemy, Lily. I am your family, and I want what is best for you."

The sound of a throat being cleared made me swivel in my chair. A man in formal attire carried a tray and a pitcher. He served us both, pouring mint tea into our glasses. When he set my plate down, I was surprised to find a hot dog, broccoli, and macaroni and cheese.

"I was told this might be something you would enjoy."

I opened my mouth a few times, staring at the plate, unsure how to respond. "Th...thank you."

The rest of the meal passed in silence as I savored the food. Honestly, it tasted better than any food I could remember. The macaroni and cheese practically melted on my tongue, sending my tastebuds into a joyous frenzy. The hot dog—oh, the incredible hot dog—I could have eaten a dozen of them and still not tired of the taste. When my plate was wiped clean, Dawn took a sip of her tea and spoke again.

"Lily, I've signed you up for tutoring to help you get your GED. The world is a cruel place for the uneducated, and I'll not allow a child of my blood to flounder when such things can be easily prevented. Secondly, I've set up a therapy schedule with Dr. Grand. She comes highly recommended in her field. Finally, if any of us are to experience any semblance of peace in the near future, we need to placate the media. I've scheduled a press conference in which you will speak to them all at once. There will be a statement prepared for you, no questions, no off-the-cuff remarks, just the facts of the matter and a demand for privacy as we recover from this ordeal."

I furrowed my brow, digesting her words. It was as though I had walked out of the woods and into an alternate universe filled with nonsense that held the key to my survival. My heart pounded with the same fear I had when I'd looked down to see the snake slithering away from me. "What about Jessica?"

"She has other obligations. It would be in your best interest to put her out of your mind. That sort of...person...

is not someone with whom you should be socializing. You'll make plenty of other friends in time."

"But—"

"I'll not argue with you, child. In this household, we do not consort with those sorts of people. End of discussion," Dawn snapped. She let her fork clatter to the table as she stood, her eyes flashing. "Now, Mrs. Mackle will walk back with you and show you how to use the intercom. I expect to see you at seven sharp for breakfast."

She was gone with a rustle of overstarched fabric before I could respond, her departure relieving some of the tension I had felt. The woman who had initially received us materialized from a different doorway and gestured for me to follow. She took me back to the cottage and showed me the basic functions of the gray box on the wall, then disappeared with a promise to come for me in the morning.

The evening stretched endlessly, and I could not get comfortable on the plush mattress. After what seemed like hours of tossing and turning, I walked out to the sunroom and settled in the wicker loveseat facing the ocean. The sky was already lightening when I finally drifted off. The sound of knocking woke me. Mrs. Mackle waited at the door wearing a sympathetic smile that showed deep in her eyes.

"It's six thirty, Ms. Andrews. I thought you might need a bit of a hand getting ready this morning." I stood there dumbly, hoping she would elaborate. "May I come in?"

"Uh, okay."

She brushed past me and motioned for me to follow. In a few minutes, I had my teeth and hair brushed, my face washed, and a fresh outfit on.

"I hope you like the clothes. I guessed a bit at the size, but my granddaughters are the ones who picked out the styles and colors. They keep up-to-date on the latest trends, not like me.

Give me a nice beige pantsuit, and I'm happy to blend in with the scenery." I looked at the elaborate design on the blouse and the high-waisted pants and shrugged. "A girl after my own heart, I see. Maybe I'll sneak out later and get a few, ah, more casual items that you might like better. Shall we go, then?"

"I'm not hungry."

"Nonetheless, you are expected. There is fresh fruit, and I believe pancakes this morning." She walked to the door and held it open. "As I remember, pancakes with strawberries were always a hit with your mother."

"You knew her?"

"I knew you both. I've been around here since the dawn of time, it seems. An old dinosaur. I watched your mother grow up. She was a good kid, a little bit wild, but a heart of gold. She was nearly the same age as my kids, and they got into all sorts of mischief around here. My, oh my. Once, she found the gardener's hedge clippers and trimmed every hedge out front into the shape of, um, an inappropriate shape. The homeowners' association was not amused. Always out for a laugh, our little Hannah."

"I miss her."

"Me, too, darling. Me, too. When she left here, everything changed, but when we lost you both, it felt like the end of the world, like I had lost my own child." She wiped a finger at the edge of her eye and smiled. "But now, we have you back. Some light in the darkness again. Maybe enough to fix what ails us all."

"It doesn't feel like that to me."

"Give it time, Lily. It takes a long time for some wounds to heal. But for now, we must get a move on. As the saying goes, time and tide wait for no man, and neither does your grandmother."

With that began the endless cycle of bending and not

breaking under Dawn's critical eye. My small rebellions—refusing meals, wandering the beach in nothing but my necklace, my stony silence when spoken to—were all met with the equally unbending steel of Dawn's backbone. She was unyielding, seemingly unaffected by my rising ire as she imposed her will upon me.

Mrs. Mackle provided welcome relief, spending her spare time showing me old pictures and telling stories about the antics of my mother. She was a kindhearted woman, and I wished she was my grandmother, not Dawn. It was clear that she had an inexhaustible well of love to draw from for me and my mother. She wasn't bothered by my quietness and never demanded more of me than I was willing to give. Her stories gave me back so many forgotten memories, reminding me of the best parts of my mother, and through them, I could feel the wounds in my heart begin to knit.

❖

I refused to speak at Dawn's press conference, standing at the back of the stage at the local park, hiding from the offending flash of cameras and shouted questions while she spoke on my behalf. Her voice was strong and sure, lifting above the crowd like a rumble of thunder. She did not speak long, and at the end, she walked off without answering a single question. Her last remark was a request for privacy. The vulturous reporters, unsatisfied with my silence, continued to call and hover around the gates of the neighborhood for weeks, hoping to catch us unaware and get their scoop. On the rare occasion that one managed to sneak down the beach, security would pounce before they got within a thousand yards of the cottage. It was baffling to know that they were there because of me.

The psychologist was much the same, though not in it for the publicity. She picked and prodded, talked endlessly about my feelings and my reactions, my relationships, my fears. I spoke little enough in our sessions that she, too, gave up and wrote me off. I was, however, content with the tutoring. I loved learning almost as much as Mr. Keim loved teaching. I raced through textbooks and literature as though they would disappear before I could finish them. I learned more words than I'd ever thought possible, more names, dates, and equations. He was a lovely man, my tutor, kind and patient, a man with a soft voice, who let my wild nature guide our lesson plans. He set us up outside as often as the weather allowed. He felt comfortable and safe, fatherly, and he managed to charm Dawn fully. After proving his worthiness with weeks of steady progress, he insisted on field trips to museums and galleries, not just to expand my knowledge, but to integrate me into the culture of a world that had grown in the years I was absent. He would sneak me through the gate hidden under blankets in his Jeep, past the few remaining reporters camped close, and show me the beauty of civilization.

My spare time was lost to the dunes and the sea, an echo of my formerly free life. I taught myself to swim in the warm blue-green waters of the Gulf, next to turtles and dolphins, among sharks and jellyfish. It was a world as diverse as the forest, with more life than I ever expected. Sand pipers, pelicans, and gulls danced on the air currents overhead.

I grew lean, powerful muscles from fighting the surf, different from the thin cords I had built in the mountains where I'd worked hard for every meal. I still struggled to make good use of the clothing, preferring the sun on my bare skin, but I did so more modestly now, covering the curves that had crept up while I wasn't paying attention. It felt odd to just drift through the days, to not have to fight for survival or worry about things beyond my control. Instead, my mind was free to wander through thoughts I'd never had time to think before.

Sometimes, I would catch my reflection as I passed a mirror, and it never failed to surprise me. More and more, I looked like the pictures of my mother that Mrs. Mackle had set up on the mantel in the cottage. Even though I had grown up over the years, I still thought of myself as the child I was before the crash and the one I'd become in the mountains. I had my mother's smile, her bright eyes and unruly blond hair. Once in a while, I thought I looked more like her than I did myself, and I wondered if I actually existed anymore.

CHAPTER NINE

Jessica arrived unexpectedly one late afternoon, picnic basket in hand. I was headed to the main house for lunch when she rounded the corner, nearly sending me off the cement and into the bushes.

"Whoops." She grabbed my wrist to steady me. "You okay?"

I must have looked as though I saw a ghost because the expression on her face turned from amusement to concern in the blink of an eye. "I'm fine," I whispered, staring at her in disbelief. "Where did you come from?"

"I was out in New Mexico doing a story on La Llorona. There's been a cluster of sightings along a few smaller creeks in one area the last two years, and a few seemed legit enough to warrant investigation. I wanted to stop in and make sure you were doing all right here. Are you?"

Not only was I shocked to see her standing in front of me, but I was very confused as to the story she told. "You were looking for pants?"

"What?"

"Those stretchy pants. Mrs. Mackle brought some for me last week."

There was a moment of silence before Jessica barked out a laugh. "No, not LuLaRoe...La Llorona, the weeping woman.

She's said to haunt waterways in the Southwest, stealing children in the night." She put her hands up and wiggled her fingers in a mock spooky gesture.

"Oh. That makes more sense."

"Is it okay that I stopped by? Dawn said I could steal you for a picnic as long as I didn't keep you out too late."

I nodded dumbly, sure that I was imagining her. The weeks she had been gone had felt like a lifetime. When she'd left, I thought it was forever. A riot of emotions, all the ones I had finally managed to smother, came roaring back to life under my skin. "How long are you staying?"

Jessica glanced briefly at the house, then at the ground. "Not too long. I have a flight to Massachusetts leaving pretty early."

We strolled across the dunes to the edge of the damp sand, where she set down the basket. "I brought a few different things since I wasn't sure what you would like. Tuna? Egg salad? I've got a turkey sandwich in here somewhere, too."

"Tuna, I guess."

She pawed around in the basket and pulled out a grape soda, tilting it toward me with a questioning look. I smiled, reaching for the bottle, closing my eyes to enjoy the sound of the carbonation as I unscrewed the cap. The first sip sent me into a coughing fit as it fizzed up into my nose.

"You gonna make it?"

"I'll live."

The conversation was sporadic and soft, as though we were just dancing around anything important that needed to be said. Soon, the sun was setting, and we wandered to the small firepit in the bare dunes behind the cottage. I grabbed a bundle of wood from the patio and lit it in the metal circle while the world grew darker around us.

"This is nice."

"Dawn had it set up after I made a fire on the beach and nearly burned down the house. That grassy stuff burns really quick. Everything is so different than on the mountain. The gardener, Hugo, brings wood for me. He knows lots of stuff about nature. He said I can't burn the driftwood because it lets toxic gases out from all the salt inside."

"You lit the beach on fire, huh? Sounds like a good time."

"They had to call the fire department. Dawn wasn't very happy."

"Is she ever?"

"Not really."

"Are things getting easier here, Lily?"

"I guess. I'm learning a lot. I get to go swimming, and Hugo taught me how to fish, but he told me not to tell Dawn because she would get mad. My teacher takes me to all sorts of places, like the museum of natural history. It was really neat."

"That's good."

"I don't have to be scared of things here. I don't have to hunt and hide and worry about getting hurt. Dawn makes me do things I don't want to."

"Like what?"

"Well, tomorrow, she is taking me to this club thing to meet her friends. She has this awful scratchy dress picked out for me to wear, and she told me I needed to go to make new friends my own age."

"You never know, you might have a good time."

"In that dress? I'll be lucky if I don't itch all my skin off before we ever get there. *Blech*."

The last streaks of sunset were fading to darkness. I looked at her, fascinated by the way the soft lines of her mouth caught the flicker of red glow from the fire. She was looking out across the water, a million miles away from me yet close enough that I could reach out and draw a finger down the side of her face. The sounds of night, the Gulf lapping the sand just out of reach, the dry grass on the dunes rustling, and the maple log being devoured by the crackling flames, filled my ears. Maybe more than my ears. It filled up my brain, overflowing and cascading through my veins until I became nothing more than a living limb of the beach. I could not turn my gaze from her as she breathed the night air in with deep sighs. I did not move closer, yet I felt her breathing me into her lungs. I imagined floating down inside her, bobbing about in the expansion and contraction of her chest.

My face flushed with a familiar heat as I struggled to resurface from the strange turn of my thoughts. She had pulled her dark eyes from the beauty of the water and fixed them on me. "Are you okay?"

I swallowed too loudly, convinced no words could possibly fall from the desert of my mouth. "Yes," I nearly croaked, clearing my throat. She leaned in, holding out a half-full bottle of soda that I drank from gratefully. "Better now."

"What are you thinking about? You look so serious."

"Nothing. Just the air."

"You're thinking about the...air? Really?"

"It, ah, it's so heavy here, like I have to carry it around with me all the time. It wasn't like this on the mountain."

"Yeah, the humidity can be a real killer along the coast. Just wait, it gets worse in the winter."

"Worse?"

"Not quite as bad as Florida, but yeah, it gets awfully sticky. Like walking through soup." The flickering light danced on her teeth as she grinned.

I raised an eyebrow while I considered drifting on a current of chicken noodle soup, holding a floppy noodle as I paddled through the hot liquid. "Sounds awful."

"Nah, you get used to it. You'll get acclimated, and soon, you won't even notice it."

"Acclimated?"

"Like, adapting. Kind of like how animals grow thicker fur in the winter and then shed in the spring. When you have a horse in a hot climate, they don't grow as thick a coat for the coldest months, but you have one in, say, Montana, and they look like woolly mammoths by October. They adapt to their surroundings."

"So I'll adapt?"

"Well, I mean, you aren't going to shed any fur, but yeah. You adapted in the mountains. Pennsylvania is a different kind of climate from Arkansas, and your body adjusted to it, right?"

"I guess. But soup sounds terrible."

"Metaphorical soup."

"Sounds even worse."

She let out a whooping laugh that startled me at first, but I couldn't help but join in. A gust of wind kicked the sand up around the edges of the firepit and blew the smoke in my face. I coughed through my giggles.

"Come sit over here, out of the line of fire." Jessica patted the sand next to her, and I slowly slid over the inches that had once separated us. Now there was nothing but a thin sliver of beach that kept our thighs from touching. The wind immediately changed direction and blew the smoke in our faces. She flopped back in the sand and laughed again. "No smoke down here."

I let myself fall back beside her. "I can't see the water now."

"But look at all the stars, Lily. It's an ocean up there, too."

I looked at the vast, cloudless night sky and immediately felt smaller. It was as though I could fade away into nothingness under a million sparkling planets, as insignificant as the grains of sand beneath me.

"Thinking those deep thoughts again, huh?"

I turned my face toward her, feeling the heat of her breath, the intensity of her attention, the shift from lighthearted conversation to something else entirely. I was no longer small and insignificant because there were just two of us in the whole universe. I didn't know how to respond, but I could not tear my gaze from hers.

"You look so different, Lily. A whole other person from the first time we met." Jessica paused as if she, too, could not find the words she needed. "Even in the picture from my trail cam, you were like a mirage. An impossibility. Nothing in the world could have prepared me for you. Seeing you for the first time, talking to you, hearing your story, it opened up a part of me that I thought was long gone. It's hard to explain."

"You're the same. I still see the sadness in your eyes."

She was silent for a bit, staring up at the drifting smoke. "You know mushrooms are all connected, right?"

"I, uh, what?" I was completely baffled. "Mushrooms?"

"Yeah. They form this network of roots that connect acres and acres of fungi in the soil. Mushrooms send messages through electrical impulses to one another through these roots." She touched the tips of her fingers to the tips of mine. "They talk to each other just like people do, only we can't hear it. My dad used to talk about it all the time, how nature talks, and we miss all of it because we don't stop to listen."

"He said the trees were singing songs."

She smiled, but the edges of her mouth wavered. "He did. He would take me into the woods behind our house, and we'd sit for hours, listening. I never heard what he heard, though. I never heard them singing."

"Me neither. But I saw them dancing in the wind, and I figured they were hearing their own songs, so maybe he was right." I didn't dare move for fear she would pull her hand away from mine.

"Oh, he was definitely right."

"How do you know?"

"Because I hear you." She looked me squarely in the eye. "At first, I only saw you from the surface, like a lonely mushroom, not the acres beneath. I didn't see the endless connections of your roots to the earth. I didn't get the messages. You weren't just the mushroom, though, Lily, you were the mountain. When I finally turned down the volume between my own ears, I could hear your song, the song of the trees, the one my dad could have spent a lifetime listening to and been completely fulfilled."

I swallowed the growing lump in my throat as she spoke. For a brief moment, I could feel myself lifting out of my body, looking down on the two of us on the dark beach. I felt her words like a gust of wind on my skin, pushing me up to the stars. My whole life before the plane crash played through my thoughts. I began to realize I had always thought of myself as the mushroom, too, without even knowing. This was the part of me that felt defective, the part that had landed me in a therapist's office so young, the part that made me different. I didn't know how to let my roots connect to the others. How could I be the mountain if I was all alone?

From my lofty view, our fingertips looked like a cord, like the roots Jessica talked about, connecting me to her. They pulsed, alive and vibrant, the first true sign of the mountain within me. I felt drenched in a giant swirl of electric joy, the likes of which I had never experienced. A fullness took hold in my chest, threatening to burst free, enormous and still growing. There wasn't enough time to ponder the depth of this before I was sucked back down into reality, to the sand and the woman who stared into my eyes as though she truly knew me.

I sat up, ignoring the smoke and drifting embers, clutching at the very edges of my control. "Why?" Jessica tilted her head behind the thin curtain of smoke drifting between us. "Why do you see that, and everyone else just sees a weirdo?"

She smiled broadly. "You aren't easy to find, Lily, not by a long shot. You've got a wall up right behind those lovely blue eyes, but that's what we do with things of value. We protect them." For a time, she looked back out over the water. "Everyone has their own thing, their own problems. Sometimes, it makes it harder to see the struggle someone else is facing. And lots of times, people are so worried they'll be rejected or give up too much of themselves if they let someone in that they just build the walls higher and wider. We stop seeing one another. We stop hearing the song. Is that what you've done?"

"I...I don't know. I never thought I was hiding." I honestly thought I was finding my own place in the world, where I wouldn't be a bother to anyone else. Was that what it meant to hide?

"It's second nature after a while. Then we get so good at it that we forget we ever tried because it becomes all we know. When I lost my father, I thought I was going to die, too. He was my whole world. I mean, I love my mom, but she has all these expectations and rigid views of what my life should look like. There's so much I can't tell her. My dad was different. He accepted me for me. With him, I never had to hide who I was."

"My dad didn't like me much, I think. He's dead, too."

"Why do you think that?"

"He didn't want to be around me. He was in the Army and was gone a lot. When he was home, he looked at me like I was an ugly bug. I thought he left because I was a disappointment."

"You don't still think that, do you?"

"No. I know it was his job. I mean, I still wonder if he was happier wherever he went than he would have been with me, but he loved my mother, and she loved him. If he had a choice, I know he would have wanted to be with her."

"It must have been hard for you both to have a relationship if he was gone all the time."

"I guess. My mother was like your father, though. She didn't want to change me or make me more like everybody else. She made things better." The fullness in my chest faded to hollow sadness. "I wish she was here."

"I know that feeling, Lily. Like a big hole opening up inside."

"Yes."

She rubbed her thumb over the back of my hand, and a little smile tugged at the corners of her mouth. "It gets better. Maybe not for a while, but you have to let it ache. I try to think about all the wonderful memories I have of my dad, and it helps a little. He was crazy, always telling these outrageous stories about things that couldn't possibly have happened."

"Like what?"

"Oh, there was this one time, he told me our dogs could talk. He would sit and have whole conversations with them, letting them 'whisper' in his ear. For a whole year, he had me convinced that our Lab wanted to go to school to be a dentist, and the golden retriever came from a long, distinguished line of kings." She rolled her eyes. "I was eight at the time, and boy, did my friends make fun of me. Crystal still brings it up now and again when we get together."

"You actually believed they could talk?"

"Uh, yeah. I was eight. I thought the world was magical and my toys came to life when I slept. It wasn't a stretch to picture my dog in a white coat filling some bald guy's teeth. I did wonder about how he would hold the drill." She tapped her chin and winked at me. Her other hand continued to warm my own, distracting me from the soft flow of conversation.

I gnawed the edge of my lower lip, totally focused on the journey of her thumb across my knuckles. This was yet another new feeling, one that started at my toes and tingled upward, causing me to shiver slightly.

"Cold? Do you want to head inside?"

I shook my head and lay back down, giving my body up to the tingling. She slipped her hand from mine and propped herself on her elbow, looking down at me. Half her face was hidden in the shadows.

"I can't believe I'm here. It feels like another fairy tale. The magic kingdom by the sea, the beautiful princess, the light of a zillion stars. If I were writing this story, the next scene would be the happy ending." She dropped backward and sighed. "Such a shame."

"You don't like happy endings?"

"Everyone does. It's just—"

The beam of a flashlight blinded us both. "Lily, isn't it past time you retired for the evening?"

Jessica scrambled to her feet at Dawn's words. "Sorry, ma'am." The fire hissed out as she doused it with a bucket of water.

"Perhaps I wasn't clear about the rules of our little agreement, young lady. If you plan on continuing these visits, you will ensure that they do not interfere with the schedule of the day. Lily needs to be well rested for tomorrow."

"Ah, I didn't realize how late it was. I apologize for keeping her."

Angry to be treated like a child, I interrupted forcefully. "But I'm *not* tired."

"Nonetheless, it is time for our guest to be on her way."

Dawn stood ramrod straight, clenching her jaw at my refusal to budge.

"It's okay, Lily. I've got a flight to catch in a few hours anyway, so I really should be heading back to the hotel." As she walked up the dunes toward her car, I imagined the tendrils of my roots reaching for her.

"Why can't she stay here? Why did you make her leave?" I could feel myself sliding back into childhood, complete with pout and stomping foot.

"We will discuss this further at breakfast." Dawn turned and walked off toward the main house, even her clothes stiff and unyielding in the night breeze.

CHAPTER TEN

M orning arrived, a bright and beautiful one, at that. Despite the gorgeous weather, I was irritable and sluggish. I skipped breakfast, earning a sour look from Dawn, but she would not allow me to skip the brunch at her beloved country club. Mrs. Mackle helped me put on the awful white dress peppered with lace and bows, over an equally uncomfortable bra that pinched my shoulders. I picked at the fabric and scowled as we pulled out of the driveway for the ten-minute journey.

"Why did you make Jessica leave?"

"I thought we had settled all this nonsense, Lily."

"No, you said we would talk about it at breakfast."

"And perhaps we would have, if only you had shown up."

She turned away from me and looked out the window, refusing to engage in any further conversation. I was infuriated and exhausted by the time we arrived at the country club.

"Stand up straight, Lily." She brushed an invisible speck off the dress before we stepped into the lobby. "There. Now, remember, you need to be on your best behavior. The Hamiltons are a very well-respected family, and I want them to see what a nice young lady you've become. Besides, you never know when you might stumble across a handsome gentleman." Her smile was unsettling, as though she was enjoying some secret joke at my expense.

We crossed the open lobby, past a giant fountain with a statue of three golfers shading their eyes and pointing. The ceiling was so far up, I couldn't imagine a ladder tall enough to change the light bulbs on the crystal chandeliers. I wanted so badly to hate the ornate walls and pale, checkered carpet, but it was actually quite beautiful. The dining room was up a half staircase, one of its walls made entirely of windows that showed part of the immaculate golf course. Everything was huge and open. The soft voices of a few diners echoed gently. I homed in on one conversation that rose a bit above the others, an older woman and a young man who sat near the windows.

"I wish you'd shave that dreadful thing off. You look like a homeless person."

"Gee, thanks, Gram." The young man stroked the downy-looking reddish fuzz growing on his chin. "I don't remember you putting up this much of a stink when John grew a beard."

The old woman sighed with disgust. "Your brother is very well-kempt with distinguished facial hair and a nice haircut. You, on the other hand…Oh, never mind. It's too late to worry about that now." She turned slightly and caught sight of us walking toward her table, her eyes widening. She turned back to her grandson. "Good Lord, Charles, tuck your shirt in, at least. They'll think we've raised a heathen."

"You have, Gram. A heathen with undistinguished facial hair," he replied, rolling his eyes.

I tried my best not to laugh at her feigned surprise when we reached their table. That poor kid with her probably felt as out of place here as I did. He swept his long red hair behind his ears and stood, not bothering to tuck in the loose tails of his white shirt.

"Lily, this is Maureen Hamilton. Maureen, my grand-daughter, Lily Andrews."

"Dawn, how nice to see you again. I'm so glad to finally meet you, Lily. What a lovely dress. Welcome to the club. This is my grandson, Charles. He'll be joining us for our meal today. He's a freshman at Texas A&M." We all stood in awkward silence for a few seconds before she pursed her lips and puffed out her cheeks. "Charles, please assist Lily into her chair."

He stepped over and pulled out a chair for me, leaning to whisper in my ear as I sat. "Don't mind my Gram. She's an acquired taste, if you know what I mean. She'll talk your ear off if you let her."

I mumbled a thank you and sat. After we ordered, the conversation consisted mainly of Maureen firing questions at me and talking all about Charles and his accomplishments. Dawn sat back and chewed her food without a word, allowing Maureen to chatter away until the empty plates were removed. Then she cleared her throat and pushed back her chair. "Perhaps Charles would like to take Lily on a tour of the property. Is that all right with you, dear?"

Maureen snapped her mouth shut and nodded at Dawn's question, pushing back her own chair as well. "Oh, most certainly. It's a lovely day for a walk." She smiled that same awful smile Dawn had when we arrived, then fluttered her hands at Charles and winked.

He rolled his eyes and smiled at me. "I could use some air. How 'bout you?"

I looked at the three of them and shrugged, unsure what the nonverbal conversation between them was all about.

Charles led me by the arm down the short staircase and out the front door into the sunshine. Once we were away from the other two, he rolled his shoulders and sighed. "Sorry about that. They're about as subtle as a cement truck. Now that we aren't being studied, we can actually talk like normal people. How about we start again?" He held out his hand. "I'm Charlie, but all my friends call me Rip."

"Why Rip?"

"I, ah, I've never been very good at keeping my clothes nice. Every time I put something on, I manage to tear it somehow." He pointed to his pant leg and a small tear at the knee. "I'm told regularly that this is why I can't have nice things."

"Maybe we should both be called Rip." I pointed at the lacy flap at the side of my dress that I'd managed to pull loose in the car, and we both started to laugh.

"I'll be Rip One, and you can be Rip Two."

"Sounds good to me."

The rest of the afternoon passed quickly as Charlie and I walked the grounds of the country club. He was friendly and funny, so very unlike our grandmothers. He let me volunteer information but didn't pry into my past. I learned about his family and his friends at school, where he studied microbiology. When I told him about living on the mountain, he listened with a look of awe on his face, especially when I talked about Biscuit.

"I know that feeling when you find a friend like him. My brother, John, raises coonhounds. A few years ago, he had a runt that wasn't doing so hot, so I took him home with me. He's been my wingman ever since. Big ugly guy with a bit of an underbite and a ten-ton noggin, but he's got a heart of gold and a brain of pudding. Maybe I'll bring him out to see you one of these days, if that's all right with you."

"What's his name?"

"Mako, like the shark. Nothing but teeth and speed. Poor guy doesn't know how to hit the brakes once he gets running. Just turns sideways and slams into whatever he finds."

"Mako. I like that."

We walked back up to the main building as the lights outside clicked on. Both Dawn and Maureen were sipping drinks on the patio. "It's so nice to see you two hitting it off. We should plan another get-together soon, right, Charles? Perhaps take in a play or take the yacht out for an afternoon?"

I squirmed uncomfortably under her stare, aware that there were plans being made all around me, and I had no say in anything. At least Charlie was down-to-earth and easy to talk to. There were worse friends to have, I was sure.

❖

The next few weeks were filled with lessons, little trips with Charlie, Maureen, and Dawn, and very little free time. From the moment I awoke, my day was planned and executed with military precision. It seemed Dawn was determined to fill every moment I was not sleeping. She dragged me to luncheons, charity events, and polo matches, draping me on Charlie's arm at every opportunity. He was a good sport, playing the role of escort with a lazy smile and a half bow every time we met.

After one particularly boring dinner, we walked out onto a huge stone patio to escape the eagle eyes of our grandmothers. "Is this what it's like to have a brother?" I asked.

He wrinkled his nose. "Uh, no. Why would you ask that?"

"Oh. I just meant having someone to talk to and stuff. Growing up with someone your age."

"I dunno. John is, like, fourteen years older than me. We were never close. And I never wanted to kiss him." He stepped closer to me, leaning in as I tilted away.

"What are you doing?"

"I was going to kiss you, but, ah, you're looking at me like I have a booger."

"Why?"

"I was going to ask you the same thing. I don't have a booger, do I?" He brushed his hand across his nose a few times and laughed.

"No. I meant, why were you going to kiss me?"

"Because I like you. I thought you liked me. Isn't that why we're here? On the balcony? In the romantic evening light?"

"I thought we came out here to get away from them." I hiked my thumb toward the two women who were sitting near the windows sipping champagne.

"Hmm. Okay, I don't think we're on the same page, are we? I really like you, Lily. And not because those two set it up. You're cool, you're beautiful, you laugh at my stupid jokes."

"Your jokes aren't stupid. Well, not all of them, anyway."

"Harsh. Way harsh. Next, you're going to tell me you don't think I'm cute, aren't you?"

I raised my eyebrows at him, completely lost.

He clutched his chest and pretended he was going to fall to his knees. "Damn, kid. Just keeping those hits coming, aren't you? I guess I thought you were as into me as I am you."

"I'm sorry." I stared at my feet, uncomfortable around him for the first time.

"Nah. It's fine. I'm a big boy. I didn't ruin it, did I? You look like you're ready to bolt." He reached out and pulled the knit shawl up over my shoulder. "I promise, I'm not one of *those* guys. I'd rather have you as a friend than not at all."

"Is that the only reason you talk to me?"

"'Cause I'm into you? No. I talk to you because you're interesting. You have more interesting things to say than anyone I've ever met. You're, like, my hero with all the stuff you've done. I'd never have survived out there. I don't know anyone who would've, honestly. I'm glad those two meddling old broads introduced us. Spiced up life a bit, didn't it?"

"Yeah, I guess."

"We can still hang out, right? Don't worry, I won't tell our grandmas their evil plans have been foiled."

"Evil plans?"

"Yup. Us hooking up, getting married, spawning a new generation of rich kids to carry on the family flaws, staring at our grandchildren with a sour look of disapproval when they dare to try growing a beard. The usual stuff."

"That sounds awful. Is that what you want?"

"I don't really think that far ahead. I mean, I want to finish school, find a cushy job where I can stare into a microscope all day, and enjoy some bangin' fried chicken every once in a while. That's it. That's my whole plan. After that, I'll let the big man upstairs take the reins. How about you? What's your plan?"

"I want to go back to the mountains. Not in the cave but in a real house. I want to have a dog and a pair of binoculars for bird watching and a big garden. Oh, and some fried chicken sounds good, too."

"All by yourself?"

"No." I turned away and faced the lawn below, squinting into the darkness to see the fountain that gurgled away.

"Oh. *Oh.* You already have someone in mind, don't you? It's okay, you don't have to tell me." He made a motion like he was buttoning his lips.

I wanted to like him more. I wanted to want what he wanted, but no matter how hard I tried, I couldn't quite make those pieces fit together. "Sorry."

"You gotta stop apologizing for being you, Lil. You just keep being your awesome self and let the world learn to deal. We all deserve to chase our own dreams, right?" He took my hand and led me back inside, charming as ever while we mingled under the brightly lit chandeliers.

❖

Charlie and I shared some of the same interests, especially wildlife. When he offered to take me to an aviary to see the exotic birds, I was thrilled. Dawn was even more excited at the thought of us taking a day trip alone. She spent the day before fussing over what I would wear and how I would do my hair. It was excruciating. In the end, she relented, and I was able to leave with a tank top and cutoffs, though she did manage to pull my unruly mane up into a clip. At least it kept the thick mass off my neck in the summer heat.

Charlie arrived in an ancient Chevy Nova painted iridescent blue. He hopped out and ran to open my door for me, ever the gentleman, waving at Dawn, who kept watch from the porch.

"Your chariot, milady," he announced, bowing as I climbed in the passenger seat. Once he trotted around to the other side and hopped in, he turned to me and smiled. "I hope you don't mind, but I invited someone along for the fun. We're meeting up there."

"That's fine. I can't wait to see this place." I was thrumming with anticipation at seeing the birds. He had shown me pictures of some of them on his phone a few days ago, and they were magnificent. I counted off twenty different species in my head and tried to imagine what they would look like close up.

It took nearly an hour to get there, and we chatted about the life of parrots most of the way. I was engrossed in our conversation as we parked, lost in my train of thought, oblivious to our surroundings. Charlie cleared his throat, pointing toward the entrance, and I skidded to a stop, shocked to see who was leaning against the low stone wall.

"How…" I was at a loss for words.

"I did a little snooping, and I figured that was the Jessica you mentioned when we talked. I thought it would be nice to invite her along, ya know, get the band back together and whatnot." He offered a mischievous grin as he shrugged and put his hands up. "Seriously, though, I know I should have asked first, but I thought it would be a nice surprise. It's okay, right? Or am I being a total shithead and reading the room wrong again?"

I was still too stunned to respond. After our last encounter, I was sure Dawn had chased her off for good. Jessica wore a pale blue polo shirt and jeans, a Carolina Panthers ball cap, and a pair of worn hiking boots. As she caught my eye, the paper coffee cup she had been sipping from slipped from her hand.

"Shit." The steaming liquid splattered along the hem of her jeans and the top of her boots as the empty cup skittered across the sidewalk toward me. She leapt forward and snatched it up just as it reached my feet. I could feel my chest constricting as she stood, blushing. I looked back at Charlie, positive this was nothing but a vivid dream.

"Boy, Texas sure does look good on you," she murmured, almost too low for me to hear. She leaned in and gave me a quick hug but pulled away before I could return it. "How have you been, Lily?"

Nothing came out as I moved my lips. I had a thousand things I wanted to say, and all I could muster was a weak smile as the hammering of my heart drowned out all the words. I realized that what I truly wanted to do was to kiss her. I dropped my gaze to her full lips, imagining the feel of them against my own. She took a step backward.

Charlie hung back for a moment, then stuck out his hand. "S'up, Jess."

"Hey. Nice to meet you in person, dude. You look

absolutely nothing like your profile pic." She shook his hand, then plucked the sunglasses off her cap and put them back on.

"Uh, it's a petri dish."

"I know. You look nothing like it."

He snorted with laughter. "I'll take that as a compliment."

"Thanks for the invite."

"No prob. How was the trip down?"

"Up, actually. Honduras."

"You really get around, don't you? Must be quite a life."

"At times. Sometimes, it isn't all it's cracked up to be." I could feel her eyes on me despite the dark glasses. "Shall we go in? I need to hit the restroom to clean off this damn coffee." She gestured to the dark spots on her boots.

I followed her into the bathroom, not wanting to lose sight of her for fear she might disappear once more. As she rubbed a wet paper towel across the stains, I leaned against the counter and watched. When she finished, she washed her hands, then reached over and touched one of the curls that flopped out of the clip struggling to keep my hair contained.

"You look different with your hair up. It's like seeing you for the first time again. Like every time I see you, you've morphed into something even more beautiful than the last time. I don't know how that's even possible."

"I haven't changed."

"You've done nothing but change. It's good, though. You look like you're finding your place in life." She acted as though she was going to say something else, then changed her mind. "Well, we better not keep your friend waiting. He seems pretty keen to show us around this place." I followed her back out to where Charlie waited.

The aviary was the main focus of the building, but there were several other habitats with reptiles and small mammals.

The first area we walked into was more of an art gallery. Hundreds of blown-up photographs of birds lined the walls, with placards of information underneath them. We spent a while checking them all out, then moved into the actual bird habitat, which was enormous. I was instantly overwhelmed by the beauty of the place, walking in front of my friends on the long, latticed metal ramp that led to the high catwalk.

Charlie and Jessica chatted while I stared into the trees. The palms and rubber trees hid birds that cawed and squawked overhead, invisible except for the rustling of leaves. Occasionally, a flash of bright red feathers would appear, or a vibrant blue bird would whoosh from one tree to the next. The rush of water dashing against rocks along the banks of the small stream below the catwalk left the air misty and thick. It was cacophonous in the glass dome, nearly drowning out the sound of some of the smaller birds singing lustily from their perches.

As we walked down the stairs onto the cement path, my heart caught in my throat. The fern fronds beside us trembled, then parted, and just like the mural on the wall of my childhood therapist's office, a peacock appeared. In that moment, I felt the past clawing at my shoulders, sucking me backward with such force that it felt as if the world was collapsing around me. My vision became a pinpoint of light focused around the iridescent feathers on the regal bird's head as he bobbed onto the path. I could hear my name being called faintly somewhere behind me, then there was nothing, not the rush of water, not the calls of the songbirds and parrots, not the sound of the crowd around us remarking over the beauty of the habitat.

I didn't know how long I was trapped in the whir of memories, but the warmth and squeeze of arms encircling me slowly brought me back from the abyss. The earthy scent of Jessica filled my senses when I sucked in a deep breath. I opened my eyes to her face inches away, concern furrowing her brow.

"Hey, there, kiddo. You back with us?" Her voice was a low rumble in my ear, soft and soothing against the sandpaper edges of my emotions. Her arms remained tight around me, supporting my weight as I sagged forward.

I nodded slightly and closed my eyes to block out the harsh sunlight beating down through the glass ceiling. Her embrace was a balm to my frazzled mind, a safe harbor from stormy thoughts and painful memories. I counted her breaths, using them to find a tempo for my own, easing the constriction around my aching, pounding heart. It might have been the panic of the moment or her scent or the feel of her hands stroking my back; whatever it was, it zinged along my muscles, drawing them tight as a bowstring. A flush of heat crashed through me like a rogue wave.

Charlie came running toward us, staff member in tow, gesturing wildly in my direction. "Ma'am, are you okay? Do you need medical attention? I can call for an ambulance or something," the employee said, puffing slightly from his run.

"I think we're all right, just need to find someplace quiet to take a breather, right, Lily?" I nodded against her chest, afraid to look up as she guided me toward the exit and into the darker corridors of the building. There were benches along a curving, glass-walled tree frog exhibit, and the three of us sat for a while, listening to the sounds of the rainforest being piped in through the speakers.

"Dude. That was kinda intense, huh? Like, what happened? You were standing there smiling, then all of a sudden, it looked like someone just flipped a switch. Man, I thought you were gonna hit the deck." Charlie looked at me from his perch on the edge of the bench, waiting for a response.

"I don't know," I mumbled, staring at the gray pebbly floor, ashamed and confused about my reaction. There was so much I had forgotten about my childhood, so many memories, so many feelings. The peacock had brought back a vivid image of my mother resting her chin in her hand as she spoke to the doctor. It had even brought back the smell of her perfume, the texture of her hand in mine as we'd walked down the hall, the feel of my sneakers on the flat beige carpet, all the things I had not experienced in years.

"You know, my mom used to have the same thing happen to her. She worked in the ER for years and ended up with some pretty bad PTSD from the things she had to deal with. It took a long time for her to be able to find her triggers. She had some wicked panic attacks. We used to sit in the bedroom closet, hugging, waiting for the worst of it to pass." Jessica's voice was hushed, soft as a marshmallow in my eardrums. She still had an arm around my shoulders as I leaned into her.

"PTSD is no joke, man. My brother came back from Iraq with it. Makes sense." Charlie patted my knee and gave a little smile. "It took John a helluva long time to come to grips with all the things he saw over there, but a part of him always struggles. A good support system helps a lot."

"Maybe we should call it a day?"

"No, I'm fine. Don't go." I couldn't hide the edge of pleading in my voice when Jessica stood.

"Lily, I…" She brushed a tear from my cheek. "I need to get back, anyway. Deadlines to meet and other stuff to take care of. I'll call you tomorrow, okay?"

It was not okay. It seemed like every little bit of time I had with her was snatched away before I had my fill. Instead of watching her walk away, I followed her down the corridor and grabbed her hand. "You always run away from me."

"I'm not running from you." She turned her head and

looked back in the direction from which we came. "Charlie is a good guy, nice, handsome, even with that crazy red scraggle he calls a beard. Don't let him get away."

"What?"

"He'll take good care of you, you know. He's sweet. Go with him."

"I don't want to go with him. I want to go with you."

"Lily, I don't know what you want from me, but I know it isn't the same as what I want. I can't be that person for you, the one who stands by and watches you grow into the person you should have been while I'm just the same old damaged third wheel. Whatever this is"—she gestured in a circle between us—"whatever you think this is, it can't be. Dawn made it clear that I am not welcome in your life, that I should keep my distance. I can't. Whenever I'm near you, I can barely think. I swear, every time I see you, it gets harder and harder to remember that you just walked out of the woods."

"You don't get to tell me what I want. You and Dawn and Maureen and the whole world keep trying to shove me into a life that doesn't fit."

"I'm not trying to force you into anything. Quite the opposite, in fact. I'm trying to save you from…me."

"Why would I need saving from you? You wouldn't hurt me."

"No, I would never intentionally hurt you. Never."

"I don't understand. Why would I need saving from you, then?"

"Because you've led this sheltered life, and I don't want to be the one to…You have so much to look forward to, so many firsts, so much time to find out who you are and what you want to be. I already know who I am. Life is going to be full of new experiences for you, and I don't want to be the one tugging on the leash and holding you back." She blew out a heavy breath. "The only real thing I can offer you is time to grow up." Jessica looked back to where Charlie lounged on the bench just out of earshot. She worried at the end of her braid with quick, unsteady fingers.

"If you want to leave so bad, why do you keep coming back?" My voice was barely a whisper, sticking to my tongue and clinging to the backs of my teeth, fighting to stay inside.

She dropped her head into her hands and chuckled grimly. "Masochistic tendencies, I suppose. Just another member of the U-Haul army setting my sights on the unattainable. I wonder if they have a support group for that."

She was infuriatingly confusing. What did any of that even mean? I gritted my teeth as I watched her pull and flick the tuft of hair sticking out below the blue hair tie. I grabbed her hands with both of mine and looked directly into her eyes, finding unfathomable depths that held more than she would ever choose to reveal. "Stay."

She brushed her lips gently against my cheek and stepped back, eyes shining in the dim light. "We both know I can't. Better things are waiting for you." She gestured toward Charlie, who smiled as I turned to look.

When I turned back, there was nothing but empty space and heartache in her place. I stood there for a long time, trying to hold back my tears. When a gentle hand touched my shoulder, I jumped, forgetting Charlie was still there.

"It's her, right?"

I looked at him sideways, trying to decide what answer he wanted.

He smiled broadly and put an arm around my shoulder. "*I knew it.* I could see it in your eyes the minute you saw her standing there. That was some serious chemistry. Man, I should do this for a living. I could call myself the Matchmaking Microbiologist and make a mint." I started to sob, and he folded me in his arms. "Come on, don't cry, Lil. I can't stand to see you cry."

"I'm sorry," I hiccupped, unable to stem the flow of my misery.

"Ah, let's get out of here. We can still make it to the club for happy hour. They make a mean Shirley Temple we can drown our sorrows in."

❖

The drive back to the club was made in complete silence. Charlie reached across the front seat and held my hand as I stared out the window, forlorn. He led me past the main foyer to a cozy room with plush couches and felt-lined pool tables. We sat away from the windows near the empty fireplace, far out of reach of any prying ears. There were only a few older men in the room, anyway, reading the paper and talking amongst themselves about some sports team heading for the playoffs.

Charlie laid his arm along the back of the couch as he squinted thoughtfully. "We should definitely talk about this. This is a big thing."

"What is?" I looked away, chewing on the skin at the edge of my fingernails.

"Uh, you being, you know..." He looked around and leaned closer. "Gay."

I gnawed harder, peeling back a layer near my cuticle that gave way to a drop of blood. I watched the red bead well up, nearly as dark as the red carpet in the room. If it fell from my finger to the floor, no one would even notice. I considered what it might be like to be that drop of blood on the vast carpet, to disappear from view and never have to answer any of the hard questions everyone around me always seemed to have.

"Lil, come on. Talk to me. I want to make sure you're okay because you *really* do not look okay right now."

I didn't feel okay, either. "I don't know what you want me to say."

"Be honest with me. Tell me what you're feeling. Let me in a little."

"I don't know how."

"That's part of the problem, I think. Can I ask you something crazy personal?"

"I guess."

"Did you know you liked girls, or is this something new?"

I considered his question, working through my memory methodically. "I don't know if I ever thought about it, really. I've never felt like this before. What does that mean?"

"It means you fell in love. We don't get to pick the people we fall in love with. That person isn't always the one we thought we'd find, and the people around us don't always understand or appreciate those feelings, but don't let it bug you. Haters gonna hate, am I right?"

"She doesn't like me back."

"*Ha.*" Charlie rolled his eyes and shook his head. "I may be totally oblivious to, like, ninety percent of the crap other people are feeling, but I know the look she was giving you, my friend. That was *not* a look of someone who doesn't like you back. That girl is way into you. If I find someone who looks at me even half as intensely as she looks at you, I'd consider myself one lucky bastard."

"You think so?"

"I know so. That's like, Westley and Buttercup kind of love, right there."

"Who are they?"

"Who are...Has no one shown you *The Princess Bride*?"

The look on his face was a cross between shock and complete dismay.

"No."

"Inconceivable! It is literally the greatest movie ever. Ever. What is that tutor teaching you? Obliviously nothing worthwhile. That's it. It is now my life's mission to expose you to the world of cult cinema."

"I'm sure that'll be far more useful than E equals MC squared," I replied dryly.

"Such sass from you. You'll see. When I'm done with you, you'll be able to spot true love from a mile away. Way more useful than that dusty old theory of relativity stuff, if you ask me."

"And what good will that do me? Jessica will still be gone." The crushing weight of my despair descended once more, pushing me deep into the plush couch.

"We'll see about that. The Matchmaking Microbiologist has a few more cards up his sleeve, fear not." He winked and put a hand on my shoulder. "But seriously, though, I'm here for you no matter what. Besties, right?" He put his hand up in the air, wiggling it to get my attention.

I gave it a half-hearted slap. "Besties." Silently, I wished I had a single shred of his optimism.

CHAPTER ELEVEN

There were days when I felt rebellious and wild, days where I fought tooth and nail for a chance to be alone. I would lie on the beach and remember the feel of Jessica's fingertips on mine, the connection we had under the ocean of stars. I would reach out, lay my hand on the cool sand, and dig my fingers in, hoping to find the roots that connected us.

She called every few days, checking in, she would say, making sure I was still the same wild woodswoman she had first encountered. She would tell me of the strange places she visited for her stories and the even stranger people she encountered along the way. I told my story in bits and pieces, like a breadcrumb trail, never seeming to find enough words for her to find her way to me. Sometimes, she asked me to read from the journals I had brought back. Sometimes, she would throw me for a loop with odd questions about the feel of striking my fire rocks together or the smell of pine needles after the rain or the sounds of the forest when the snow fell.

When our conversations grew stilted and the words had stacked between us once more, she would hang up, and I would feel the same growing void as the day she had left. By August, I dreaded the calls, not because I didn't want to talk to her, but because I would have to lick my wounds for hours after, sending me to bed heartsick and troubled. The last week of the month came and went without a word, which, it turned out, was even *worse* than taking the call in the first place.

I moped around the cottage, turning away Mr. Keim and Mrs. Mackle, turning away my grandmother when she insisted it was mealtime, turning away from the beach and folding up inside myself for comfort. Dawn dragged me out of the house to the dentist, to a doctor, to visit Charlie. Even his easy humor and endless collection of quirky films could not pull me out of the funk I was in.

Days felt like years. The clock on the mantel ticked so slowly, I was sure it had stopped completely. I stared at it more and more, wishing away hours because I no longer knew how to fill them.

When a soft knock on the door made me stir from the farthest corner of the couch one afternoon, I ignored it, hoping whoever it was would go away. No such luck. Mrs. Mackle poked her head inside after knocking a second and third time, then held out her hand to me.

"You've got a visitor, Lily. Someone from a long time ago, I believe."

I craned my neck to see if there was someone behind her, but she was alone. "Who?"

"No one said, but whoever it is, he seems pretty keen to see you."

"Can you tell him I'm not here?"

"I think your grandmother would disapprove of me fibbing for you."

Try as I might, I couldn't stomach the idea of Mrs. Mackle getting in trouble because of me. "I could go to the beach, then it wouldn't be a lie. Or call Charlie to come and get me."

"He's been here and gone already today. He keeps checking in to make sure you're okay. He doesn't want to pester you when you say you want to be alone. Come on, sweetheart. I know you're out of sorts, and I don't know how to help you, but I do know that you can't barricade yourself in here and expect your grandmother to sit idly by. The woman is driving us crazy."

"Really?"

"She's fit to be tied, prowling around making poor Hugo rearrange furniture and everything. The man threatened to quit yesterday when she told him she wanted her china cabinet moved for the third time. Right back to where it started, too. Such a gentleman he is, he just clasped his hands, said a little prayer, and pushed that behemoth back before he walked out the door. I don't remember ever seeing him that particular shade of red."

"Why's she picking on Hugo?"

"Maybe because a certain granddaughter of hers has been missing in action for long enough to put her over the edge."

"I doubt that."

"Hmm. You brush that hair of yours, put on some shoes, and head up to the study. You'll see for your own eyes what a mess she is."

With that, she dipped her head and floated back out the door on a cloud of Southern Soul perfume. I grudgingly did as she asked, taming the unruly curls that had done nothing but get wilder and wilder with all the humidity, and strapped a pair of sandals on. I traipsed up to the house and followed the sound of laughter into Dawn's study, trying hard to distinguish any inkling that she was out of sorts. She sounded perfectly fine to me. I entered the study, finding a familiar stranger sitting in one of the high leather chairs.

"I didn't believe it until right now. By God, it's good to see you, Lily." Dr. Le Van leapt to his feet, staring at me as though I was a ghost.

I was sure the look in my eyes mirrored his because I felt like I was looking at a ghost as well. The last time I had seen the good doctor was our session where my mother had told him of our plans to travel south. My mouth flopped open and closed a few times as I struggled to corral my thoughts into something remotely utterable.

"You know," he said with a thoughtful expression. "I spent my whole life thinking people who believed in miracles were just reaching for hope or a sign of better things to come, grasping for straws in tough times. Now here I am looking at a real, live miracle standing in front of me, bold as brass. Sorry, I know this is probably a lot to take in. Brings back some memories, though, huh?"

I nodded and sat heavily in the chair across from him, searching through my basket of emotions for a thread of control. The doctor had aged, his hair thinner and waistline plumper. It seemed like he was shorter than ever, though it could very well have been that I was much taller than our last meeting.

"I'll leave you two to catch up," Dawn said, looking only slightly frazzled as she slipped out of the room, shutting the broad mahogany door behind her.

I squinted warily at Dr. Le Van. "Are you going to make me draw more pictures?"

He laughed. "Goodness, no. I'm not here to be your therapist, Lily. As a matter of fact, it was quite a chore convincing your grandmother to let me visit. I'm here for strictly selfish reasons. I needed to see you with my own eyes. To see that you are still the strong, resilient little girl I knew so long ago. That, and to make sure you're safe."

"I am. Safe, I mean."

"Good. You have a different look in your eyes now. Like

you've finally found the door you'd been searching for all those years ago."

"What door?"

"I don't know. I had such a hard time finding you as a child. You shut down with the slightest pressure. I always imagined it like a little room you had confined yourself to where you thought you were trapped. It seemed like the door was just out of reach for everyone. Getting a word or two out of you was the highlight of my day. I thought I'd failed you both. When I heard the news of the crash, I spent a long time kicking myself for not trying to talk your mother out of leaving. It wasn't my place, really, but I still felt guilty. Maybe a little more time would have been enough to help her heal. Maybe running away was only going to prolong her suffering."

"I was a bad daughter."

"What on earth do you mean by that?"

"I didn't help her. I didn't even know she was that sad."

"You were just a child. There was nothing you could have done to make her whole again. You were the only thing that made her happy."

"But I couldn't save her. I didn't even try. Why didn't I try?" Suddenly, I was right back on the plane, tucked under her arm, listening to the sound of her shallow breathing. Why hadn't I done something to help her? What if I could have saved her? What kind of monster was I? Tears splashed onto my lap, spots of spreading darkness on the light-colored fabric. A tsunami of guilt overtook me.

"There was nothing you could have done for her, Lily. You don't have to take that on." He moved his chair closer and put a hand on my shoulder. "The fact that you survived is probably a one-in-a-million chance. She was a wonderful woman, and I know she would not have wanted you to beat yourself up over something that was completely out of your control." He pulled me into a tight hug, letting me sob against his stiff shirt.

"I just left her there," I wailed, hyperventilating. It felt like the whole weight of the plane was crushing my chest, burying me deep into the soil, suffocating me.

We stayed like that for a long while, Dr. Le Van solid and comforting, until I had no more tears to give. He wiped his eyes, too, when he finally pulled away.

"You need to show yourself a little compassion and a little forgiveness. We can't change the things that have happened to us, but you need to recognize that you're not responsible for any of the events that led to that day or the days that followed. Things happen. Accidents happen. We can't control the world around us, and we can't fix everything no matter how much we want to."

"When will it stop hurting?"

"No one can put a time frame on grief. We all have our own paths to walk. For some, healing comes quickly, for others it takes a lifetime. The thing that helps most, though, is letting yourself feel all the things that come to you. If you bottle it up, it will always be there, just under the surface, eating away at everything you build. Let it in and let it out, just like taking a breath."

"What if I can't?" The idea of spending the rest of my life feeling as I did in that moment was terrifying.

"You are capable of amazing things. Look at all the things you've gone through. All that strength I saw in you as a child is on full display. You can. I'll do what I can to help, if you want me to."

"Okay." It surprised me when it popped out of my mouth, but it felt right, like if I was going to be able to get past this, it would be with the support of someone who knew me the way

Dr. Le Van did. I felt lighter by the time he left, a little freer from the constant shadow of guilt I had been living under.

❖

On the first day of September, the sun rose and bathed the beach in a glowing halo of pinks and purples. Gulls danced on the turbulent air, and the foam-topped waves broke hard against the beach. A tropical depression hovered off the coast, threatening to make landfall in Louisiana as it twisted and spun its way over the Gulf. Lost in my funk, I had wandered deep in the dunes, plucking blades of marsh hay and tossing them into the wind to watch them flutter away. I closed my eyes and dropped to my back on the cool sand, focusing on the roar of the enlivened ocean. It took me far too long to notice the lone woman strolling along the swirling sand, braid whipping about in the sharp breeze. When I finally did, I knew she had been waiting for me to acknowledge her. I raised a hand in a brief wave, standing to brush the sand from my skin. She approached, taking her time to cross the small distance with long, lazy strides until she finally stood before me.

"Do you always lie out naked, waiting for a hurricane?" Jessica's voice was loud against the wind but seemed meant only for my ears.

"Yes." Oddly enough, it felt as though I was expecting her. The surprise I thought I should feel was absent. In its place was wariness, the sense that this would end the same as every other meeting, in a messy pile of heartbreak as she strolled off into the sunset once more. Still, I could feel my heartbeat rising and the gates of hope creaking open. Since she'd left, I'd had months cracking and drying in the drought of her, and now I felt the reprieve of her raining over me, flooding the arid plains of my soul.

She looked small against the hugeness of the ocean, and I felt somehow larger, more defined. I sensed the dynamic had changed, gifting me with the upper hand. She had only seen me at my worst, at my most vulnerable, emotional and all twisted up inside. A few short conversations with the good doctor and I'd begun to gain my footing once more, learning that strength and weakness were often mistaken for each other. The same could have been said for control and chaos. I had spent plenty of time holding each of these words up to the light and picking them apart, shoring up the cracks in my thought processes with the newly discovered pieces. It was empowering.

"Figures," she said, shaking her head. One corner of her mouth tilted wryly as she looked into my eyes.

I met her stare earnestly, searching for the borderless sorrow I'd once seen there. "What does?"

"Figures you'd be here, Venus on the half shell, lying out, awaiting the tempest." She didn't move, challenging me to look away as if amused by my defiance.

I stood my ground, remembering what Dr. Le Van had told me. I wasn't going to keep my feelings locked up any longer. *Let it in, let it out.* "You didn't call."

She broke eye contact to gaze at her shoes, swishing the sand back and forth. "I was in Brazil."

"They don't have phones in Brazil?" I could feel the muscles in my jaw clench with anger at her excuse. I wasn't letting her off the hook so easily. It had torn me to bits to think that she was tired of me, that I could be tossed aside and forgotten.

"No service in the rain forest." Her dark eyes cut sharply at me, narrowing a bit as she stared. "Gee, these last few months have made you cheeky, haven't they?"

"Why didn't you call?" Even with the hard edges of my anger clouding my view, I could tell there was something more bubbling under the surface of her words. The wind picked up, tossing stinging sand against my legs as I waited.

"Stop looking at me like that." She looked like a cornered rabbit, ready to bolt at the slightest move.

"Like what? Like if I take my eyes off you, you might vanish once and for all?"

"No, like you want to drown me in the Gulf."

I shrugged. "I'm considering it." My unexpected, light response made us both smile.

"You got your tooth fixed."

"Yes." I ran my tongue over the crown the dentist had applied. It was smoother than the rest of my teeth, the tiniest bit whiter, and I still couldn't get used to not feeling the sharp edge of the chip that I had lived with since that fateful day when the old man had saved my life.

"I don't know that I can get used to you with a perfect smile."

"I doubt you'll be around long enough for that to matter." I regretted my bitter response before the last word had left my lips, feeling the stab of my own barb as I saw the pain in her eyes.

"Yikes. Have I been that awful?"

"No. I'm just working through some things, and I'm not sure how good it is to have you catapulting in and out of my life. I'd have better odds of surviving if I took on the storm."

"I'm sorry. I didn't call because, well, I felt like we were on a different wavelength. I didn't think you wanted me to." She was a terrible liar, picking at a loose string near the button of her open flannel shirt to avoid my eyes.

I decided to keep pushing. "You know that isn't true."

"What's the truth, then?"

"I don't know. I'm still waiting to hear it." I cocked my hip and crossed my arms.

"I…You aren't going to make this easy, are you? You should put a shirt on or something. I can't have a serious conversation with you in your birthday suit. Don't you have a towel or something?" She pulled at the collar of her shirt as I raised an eyebrow, refusing to move. "*Fine.* I didn't call because I was afraid."

"Of what? Of me?" I snorted, unconvinced.

"Not of you. I was afraid you had…outgrown me. I didn't want to impose." My face must have showed my confusion. "I left because I had a lot of feelings to deal with, and being away didn't change them like I thought it would. I thought you would be better off without me bothering you all the time."

"So why are you here if that's how you feel?" The steel edge of my voice was reminiscent of my grandmother, and I could tell Jessica was taken aback by it.

She raised her hands as if in surrender, backing up a step. "Dawn called and told me you were acting 'stranger than usual.' Her words, not mine. She was concerned."

"You came because of her?"

"I came because of *you*." She tried a tentative smile. "Now, will you please put something on? I'm having a difficult time pretending not to stare at you."

Her eyes flicked down the length of my body, and I could feel them like a caress as they traveled back up. The shock wave of desire I felt nearly took me to my knees in front of her. For the first time in my life, I recognized my nakedness as something more than a personal preference. It became an invitation, an offering. The strength of it was not lost on me.

Instead of giving in to the overwhelming need to reach for her, I turned and stalked toward the cottage, trying desperately to hold on to my anger. Questions chased their tails in my brain as Jessica muttered unintelligibly in my wake. Inside, I slipped a thin cotton dress on and walked back out to the living room where she paced in front of the window, framed by thick clouds building in the east.

I could not make heads or tails of the boomerang of emotions. How could I be so angry and so sad and so elated to see her all at once? My anger dissipated as I watched her worrying away at the end of her braid. A doomed feeling washed over me as I realized that what I felt for her was unconditional love, and no matter how hard I tried to force it from my mind, it would always be a part of me. Perhaps one day, it would feel less like torture, one day when she was not standing a few feet away, devastatingly beautiful as she marched to and fro across the tile floor.

"Why so anxious?" I asked, taking the tiniest bit of joy in the fact that I had snuck up on her. She glanced at my dress and grumbled under her breath again. "What was that?" I cupped my ear and waited for her to repeat herself. She was fidgeting uncomfortably, and for some reason, it thrilled me no end to watch her flounder.

"*I said*, you might as well have left the damn thing off. It leaves nothing to the imagination." She growled softly, pointed at the lavender dress clinging to my curves.

I gave her the most innocent smile I could muster and watched her jaw tighten. "Should I change?"

"*Yes.* No. Sorry, no. I'm just a little overwhelmed right now."

I took a few steps toward her, feeling oddly in control. She backed away, wide-eyed as I reached to take the end of her braid from her hands. I rolled it between my fingers, smiling as the smell of her shampoo rose to greet me. I could see the flutter of her pulse ticking away in her jugular, speeding along, rushing the blood to her cheeks in the bloom of a blush.

"But you aren't sad anymore, are you? I don't see the line between your eyebrows," I whispered, tugging at her braid to draw her closer as I placed a finger on the smooth skin between her eyes.

She tipped forward slightly, capturing me with her dark eyes. With a sigh, she pulled back. "What are you doing, Lily?"

"Just making small talk, I guess."

"Right. Small talk. Why do I feel like I walked into an ambush today?" She slipped her hair free and chewed her lip for a moment, turning away from me. "You're right. I'm not sad anymore. My father came alive through you, through your journals and your stories. I have small pieces of him back, and he can never truly be gone if I have that, right? I feel like all these years I've been traveling just to find him, but now, I feel like I'm ready to go home. I have you to thank for that, so thank you. Thank you for letting me in."

"I didn't do anything, though."

"You did. You're still doing it. Every time I look at you, it feels like aloe on a burn, cool and healing. I'll never be able to thank you enough for that, but I do have something for you." She ran out to the car and brought a package in, handing it to me nervously.

"Should I open it now?"

"If you want."

I remembered the Christmases of my early childhood, the excitement of opening presents under the glow of twinkling, multicolored lights, the ecstasy of tearing through thin paper to uncover the secret contents. This was far different, though, and the anticipation I felt was tempered with the knowledge that this gift would be like nothing I had ever held.

The look in her eyes was hopeful but haunted, as though she expected the worst. I pulled back the flaps of the manilla envelope and released its contents in surprise. The thick sheaf of papers weighed nothing and everything at the same time. It was a manuscript titled *Lily of the Mountain* by Jessica Velasquez, with a smaller envelope clipped to the first page.

"Is this…"

"It's yours to do with as you see fit. I know I didn't really get your permission, but it wouldn't stop begging to be written, and I had to get it out of my head. I wrote it for you." Her quiet admission left my hands shaking with the heft of her burden, now released to me in Times New Roman type on crisp white pages. "You don't have to read it if you don't want to."

"I'm having a hard time not starting it right now." I tugged the smaller envelope free and looked inside, floored by what I found.

"I thought maybe this was meant more for you than for me," she said softly, looking at the watch that now dangled between my fingers. "I had the face fixed and the EcoDrive replaced. Runs like a top now."

I was completely unprepared for the tangle of grief and joy I felt as my fingers warmed the brushed stainless steel. Jack's watch. The watch that had saved my life. The watch I had thought, for sure, was lost in my flight from the cave, yet here it was, tick, tick, ticking away as though it had never been broken, never been misplaced. The beauty of that was not lost on me. Just like the watch, my wounds were mended, my breaks invisible, my life renewed.

She turned away and looked out the window. "Lily, I'm not being totally honest with you. The book isn't the only reason I'm here. I…I can't stop thinking about you. I can't sleep without you swimming around in my dreams. I can't work because every mystery I research leaves the smell of you lingering in the room. I can't even drive past a damn tree without feeling totally lost. Christ almighty, Lily, I'm a mess. How can I be this crazy for someone I barely know? It isn't rational."

"Really?" I couldn't figure out if I was feeling panic at the thought of her unhappiness or dizzy with joy that she couldn't stop thinking about me.

"Yes, really. But I don't think you get it. I mean, I can barely understand it myself. There is this great big elephant in the room every time I think of you, and it is getting harder and harder to ignore."

"Really?" It seemed to be the only word I could speak in the wake of her admissions. She liked me. Jessica liked *me*. Weeks of depression lifted from my shoulders, making me feel light as a feather.

"I mean, there is this *thing* hanging over me, waving its arms and screaming to be noticed, but I keep trying to pretend it isn't there. Over the last few months, I thought some time, some distance, would make it go away, and yet I look up, and there it is, bigger than ever, beating its way out of my chest. I even saw a therapist because I was convinced this was some super weird take on an Electra disorder or something."

"Electric disorder?" I racked my brain for any shred of context, finding nothing.

"Sorry, I've spent too much time sifting through Freud's theories for some of my work. Just some psychobabble that I latched on to in order to explain what feels like a complete and total core meltdown. Turns out, I'm not crazy, I'm just..." She smiled thinly and pinched the bridge of her nose while I waited. "I..."

The pause was long, a living, breathing being circling us like a vulture. It was a silence that felt threatening and cold, one that could do nothing but harm. I braced myself for the final rejection I feared would fall from her lips. "You?" I waved my hand to encourage her to go on, hoping she would rip her hands off my heart like a Band-Aid, quickly enough that I would die from the shock of it instead of having to wallow and suffer the way I had been.

"I think I love you, Lily." She cleared her throat and tried again. "Not a platonic...I mean, not like friends or sisters. I can't stop myself from wanting you, no matter how crazy it sounds. I think about kissing you, like, all the time."

I could feel the breath leaving my lungs in a whoosh. This was not the bad news I'd expected. This was good, wasn't it? This was what I wanted. Why did it feel like just another layer added to the agonizing pile of emotions clogging my throat? Her tone made it perfectly clear that she was unhappy with the whole idea. I couldn't follow the complex labyrinth of her discontent because I couldn't see beyond my own desires. "What's wrong with that?"

"Well." Her surprise was evident in the tilt of her head and the way her hands ceased their assault of her braid. "Well...it's just that...you aren't, you haven't...I feel like a pervert asking to take advantage of a child."

"I'm *not* a child. You're barely older than me." I could feel my anger rising again.

"Age-wise, sure, but I've had years of experiences that you never did."

"And I've had years of experiences that you never had."

"None of that had anything to do with sex!"

"So what?"

She took a step toward me, putting her hands on my shoulders as she touched her forehead to mine, breathing deeply and blowing out a ragged sigh. "The 'so what' is, I don't think you are any more ready for this than I am. Your feelings aren't the same as mine."

I gave up trying to figure out why she was in such a

state and leaned into the pressure of her skin against mine, taking whatever I could before she decided to flee. Before I could stop them, my lips rested lightly against hers, a touch so insignificant, I wasn't entirely sure it had happened. When I opened my eyes, drowning in the darkness I found staring back at me, I smiled shyly, recognizing the quickening of my heart as something other than just love, something far more primal.

Jessica tried to pull away, dropping her hands, but I would not let her go. The beat of her heart hammered against mine, the alternating softness and hardness of her body folded around me, forcing the blood to sing in my veins in new and different ways.

"Jesus, woman, are you trying to kill me?" Her voice was thick and low in my ears, sending tingles racing along my nerves and prickling the hair on my arms.

Words could not escape my parted lips; instead, they crept out the tips of my fingers as I brushed them across the back of her shirt. She arched into me, momentarily forgetting herself, closing her hands into fists over the sides of my dress. I let my body drift on the tide of these new sensations, and when her lips covered mine, the jolt of arousal was unmistakable. I let her guide me through the steps of this strange dance, opening to the gentle pressure of her tongue, sighing into the electric thrill of her hands exploring the length of my arms.

She pulled us back from the precipice, and I almost toppled over at the withdrawal of her touch. Every inch of my skin burned with a need I could not name, an ache that sank its claws into the center of me, bellowing to be freed. "Okay. This is *not* how I planned for today to go," she whispered, putting more distance between us as she snatched at her braid once more. "I thought, 'Gee, Jess, go down there, give her the book, and walk away. Let her live her life in peace and don't get involved.' What the hell was I—"

A knock on the door made us both jump. I opened it to find Dawn tapping her foot impatiently on the cement. "You missed breakfast. I thought we had—oh, I apologize. I didn't realize you had company." Her stony face softened briefly as she looked over my shoulder. She stepped around me into the cottage, uninvited. "I thank you for taking the time to visit. I'm surprised you found our Lily at home. She has a habit of wandering off."

My heart was still racing, my face still burning. "I was on the beach."

"Hopefully not as…indiscreet as usual." She turned to Jessica and added, "The gardener has been complaining about the rate at which he finds her unclothed amidst his landscaping." Her laughter was intriguing though a bit strained, a unique addition to the conversation. It smoothed her furrowed brow and took decades off her stern face.

"I thought she was a mountain lion hiding in the tall grass when I first caught sight of her," Jessica retorted, seemingly free of the turmoil I was still fighting.

"Just like her mother, tawny and wild. I could never keep that girl decent and clean. She spent her youth running naked on the beach, chasing seagulls and crabs. Sometimes, when I look out and see Lily in the surf, I forget she isn't Hannah. Of course, Hannah was a little chatterbox, always going on about things and making up stories. Lily, on the other hand, she plays her cards very close to the chest."

"There isn't much worth saying." I was irked that they spoke of me as though I wasn't in the room but more irked that I had lost the feel of Jessica in my hands. I knew I wanted more than a stolen moment, more than a brief kiss. The interruption was just one in a long line that left me frustrated and afraid. What if my grandmother used up all the time I had left with Jessica? *What if, what if, what if...* As a child, the what-ifs of the world had plagued me. I'd run through the woods fearing the next week or the next month. I was always stalked by what might come, but there was never a time where I was paralyzed by the fear of *what-if* the way I was in that moment.

"Oh, my dear, I know you have plenty going on inside that pretty little head of yours, but I think you speak a whole new language that I can't even begin to understand." Dawn's honesty was disconcerting. She glanced down and seemed to notice the manuscript on the glass end table, picking it up to flip through the first few pages before she set it back down. "I suppose, while I'm too set in my ways to learn, I should be grateful that there are others who have begun the translation." She smiled warmly at Jessica, reaching out to pat her cheek before she made her exit. The door clicked shut behind her, leaving us both stunned in the wake of her unusual behavior.

"What was that all about?" Jessica mumbled, touching her cheek as though she wasn't sure if it was still there.

I watched Dawn walk away, growing smaller in the little glass panes of the door as she strolled, not down the path to the main house but out to the beach. It might have been the loneliest thing I'd ever seen, her sleeves billowing in the wind as she stood in front of the vast gray water and frothing whitecaps. I imagined her sadness, deeper and wider than the Gulf. The same sadness I had felt. The same sadness Jessica had felt. We were a patchwork quilt of loss, stitched together haphazardly, our edges ragged against one another. Was Dawn a glimpse into my own future? Would I find myself standing at the water's edge, the hollow spot within me filled by memories that weighed no more than whispers, everything else lost to time?

I turned back to Jessica. "I think you should stay."

"It's not a good idea, Lily."

"Fuck good ideas." My curse was loud enough to startle us both, and I blushed with embarrassment. That single naughty word barreled around the room, chased by mini echoes, doubling and tripling until it seemed like the only thing I had ever spoken. I did not regret it, especially when Jessica shook her head and grinned.

"Full of surprises, aren't you?" Her wonder only lasted a moment before she let the shadows fall in her eyes once more. "I don't know if I'm strong enough to stay."

"If I can live on a mountain all alone, you can stay the night in a beach house."

She laughed at my blunt response. "Can't really argue with that logic, now, can I?" She stood near the window and smiled sheepishly.

"No." I moved next to her, wishing I could snuggle into the curve of her side as we watched the storm spin over the Gulf. Dawn was gone from the beach, leaving empty sand and surf. The weather was abating as the storm slowly crawled away from us, leaving fairer skies and calmer seas in its wake.

"There is still a lot we have to talk about, you know. That interruption didn't change my mind."

"It didn't change my mind, either." I wanted to taste her, to feel the softness of the skin I could not see. Before I could stop myself, I had my hands wrapped in the front of her shirt, pulling her toward me.

"What are you doing, Lily?"

"Why do you keep asking that? If you haven't figured it out yet, then I must be doing something wrong." I pressed my body against hers and tipped my head up.

"This is a bad idea," she murmured, staring at my lips.

"You said you wanted to kiss me."

"I do."

"I'm waiting."

She leaned in and kissed me gently, barely a touch, and it wasn't enough. I wanted her to devour me. I wanted her to tear the dress from my body and press me against the wall, taking whatever she wanted from me. Her hands were on my hips, slowly drifting upward as I squirmed. I felt her thigh between my legs, hard and warm, and I ground myself down on her jeans.

"Jesus, Lily. We should stop." Her hands rose, cupping my breasts. When she brushed her thumbs across my nipples, it was my complete undoing.

"Please," I gasped, giving myself up to the pulsing of my body.

She slid one hand down between us, pulling up the hem of my dress. I watched her eyes grow wide. "You're so wet. *Oh.*"

I could feel the pressure building, intense and throbbing as she stroked me. I let out a low moan. She pushed against me harder, matching my rhythm, pressing her face into my neck and nipping along my collarbone. The orgasm hit me like a freight train, forcing her to hold me tight so I didn't fall to the floor. Every muscle in my body contracted over and over as she covered my mouth with hers once more.

My body felt like pulled cotton, loose and airy, like I could float away with the barest of breezes. As she eased her thigh from between my legs, I sagged backward against the half wall. I looked down at the patch of wet denim, both ashamed of my inability to control myself and overwhelmed by how much I still wanted her. When she lifted her hand to her mouth, sucked her fingers, and groaned, I felt a fresh gush of desire. My mouth watered at the idea of tasting her in that way, ratcheting up my heart rate and nearly stopping my ragged breathing altogether.

"*Shit.* I'm sorry. I shouldn't have done that. I just couldn't help myself." She turned away and looked at her hands as if they had betrayed her. "Jesus, what the hell is wrong with me?"

"I wanted it."

"It doesn't matter, Lily. It shouldn't have happened. I can't believe..." She dropped onto the couch and shook her head. "You aren't ready for this."

I pointed to the wet spot on her jeans and smiled slightly. "Yeah, I think I am."

"Don't be pedantic."

"Whatever that means." I reached out and drew my fingers along the side of her face, watching the war she was fighting with herself play out in the lines on her forehead.

"How the hell did you learn to be so freaking seductive? From the minute I saw you on the beach, the only thing I've thought about is how much I wanted to touch you. I feel like you were lying in wait for me. Even now, you've got this look in your eyes, and it's making it very hard to keep my hands to myself."

"Then don't. I've had a long time to think about you over the last few weeks. A long time. I waited and waited. The more time went by, the more I thought about what I would do if I saw you."

"I thought you were angry with me?"

"Oh, I was. I still am. But there was something else, something I felt the first time I saw you and every time since. I didn't really understand it at first, and honestly, Charlie was the one who put it all into words."

"Charlie? Remind me to send him flowers or something."

I sat next to her, suddenly feeling shy. "You think I'm not ready to feel things, and I'm not ready to be a part of the world, but I am. I know exactly what I want. You."

"You don't know that. I won't be enough for you for long.

You'll soon get tired of dealing with all my issues and move on to someone more deserving."

"And what if I don't?"

"If you don't? That's a silly question. You *will*. Hell, you've only been back in the real world for a few months, and you're already more well-adjusted than I am. It's only a matter of time before you realize that, too."

"I didn't know you were a psychic. Anyone ever investigate that, or is it just another unproven legend?" I asked.

"Ha ha. Very funny."

"So you aren't a psychic? Well, then. How can you know the future? Seems like the only reasonable answer is that you don't."

"Must you be so logical all the time?"

"I guess one of us should be, right?"

She shook her head again and sighed. "Fine. I'll stay for a little while."

We wasted the rest of the afternoon with a walk on the beach, a quiet lunch in the cottage, and the rare brush of her hand against mine, stolen moments I would cherish. We did not talk about the future or the past. The breeze captured the few words we spoke, pushing them out to sea. I imagined them floating on top of the water, drifting closer and closer to the storm that had all but disappeared on the horizon. The words would catch on towering waves and surge toward the opposite shore, letters breaking away from one another until there was nothing but consonants and vowels left stranded in little tide pools on the sandstone. Starfish and hermit crabs would creep closer and closer, munching the crisp edges and curved lines, devouring every wisp of conversational remains.

Dinner was a casual affair for once, with Dawn conjuring up a picnic on the veranda. She and Jessica exchanged small talk, awkward but friendly, filled with the light humor of bygones newly at rest. As I munched placidly on my fried chicken and greens, they opened doors for one another, allowing a sliver of sunlight to grow between their opposing personalities. The softening of Dawn was the single most humanizing thing I had ever witnessed, changing her from stiff and haggard to a graying version of the beautiful woman who had raised me, a mirror to what my mother would have been had she lived to see her seventies.

CHAPTER TWELVE

The evening grew, pressing shadows like flower petals on the sidewalks and pooling under the palm trees. The September air held a slight chill, enough to chase us from the veranda into our respective domains. Jessica and I walked the path to the cottage in companionable silence, closing out the world after we crossed the threshold. I turned to her, fearing that whatever I hoped for would not be. I could not say the words out loud; in fact, I could not even pick them up and carry them with me because they were heavy and awkward.

I love you, I screamed inside, praying she would hear the echoes of my thoughts. Instead, she wished me good night, and her bedroom door clicked shut with an air of finality. I waited outside of it for a time, debating whether I should knock, knowing that even if I was welcomed in, it would only grow the hurt. In the end, I just pressed my fingertips to the wood and turned away.

Still wide awake and boiling with the need to open the first page of her manuscript, I parked myself on the sofa to read by the light of the full moon that glowed as bright as daylight across the water. It was incredible, this retelling of my short time on Earth. The characters were painfully familiar, brought to life so well, my heart broke over and over again as I flipped each page. It was written as if Jack was the narrator, his voice a

• 209 •

clear and chiming bell over every event. She showed the tough old man and his dog to be white knights, laying down their swords for their queen. She gave herself the status of bumbling interloper, too fixated on her goals to see the kingdom around her but much loved by her narrating father, who waxed poetic on the lonely growth of his only child.

The book told of my wild flight from the snake who could have ended me, the campers who'd helped, and the nurse who'd loved me despite my shortcomings. Jack's voice hummed in my ears, captured so well by his daughter that it truly felt like his own.

The last few pages were not the ending I expected but a beginning, filled with hopefulness and opportunity. On the very last page, opposite the final paragraph that ended in ellipses, was a poem she had handwritten. Her words filled me with longing and cracked me wide, exposing the raw center of what it felt to love and be loved.

> *I was asleep for years till you ventured near,*
> *Till your breath stirred my pulse, my eyes were unawake.*
> *Then, in them grew fire, a blaze that lit me like dry tinder.*
> *It crackled the length of my new livened skin,*
> *And danced in froth filled veins,*
> *Till my heart squeezed out its very first beat.*

Morning streaked across the sky as I turned her work over in my hand, unable to let it free of my grip. I was moved beyond measure by the tenderness she had showed my story. It was my life written on these pages, but it felt new and different through someone else's eyes, and when I saw myself in it, I was shocked at the truth of what I had endured. I cried more reading those pages than I had in the entirety of my life on the mountain. I could feel the badge of bravery she had pinned upon me unjustly. I had survived not because I was special but on the generosity of strangers, both human and animal. My heart ached to know she thought so many things of me that I could not see: strength, determination, endurance, intelligence. Her words painted me the hero when I was just an ordinary girl in extraordinary circumstances.

The sky had blossomed into full morning while I stared out the window at the Gulf. Jessica cleared her throat beside me, startling me. Her hair hung thick and loose down her back, shining in the sunlight that beamed through the window. It made her look young, vulnerable, and untouchably beautiful. She glanced at the pages in my hand, then squeezed her eyes shut as she took a deep breath. "I kinda hoped I would be hundreds of miles away when you read that. You finish it?" She gathered up her hair, rolling it back and forth between her fingers while she rocked from foot to foot nervously.

"Yes." I handed the manuscript to her, watching her hands flutter across the title page, holding it as if it was a loaded gun.

"Oh." She scrutinized my face, searching, it seemed, for any sign of how I had taken it, but I offered her nothing. "I'm sorry."

"For what?"

"I did the best I could, but…"

"It was good. Better than good. I spent my life up there, and I feel like I'm just now figuring out who I was. Who I *became*. That seems wrong somehow, that it took someone else's words to…I don't know. I can't explain it. I read this, this girl's tragic story, and it's like I'm experiencing it for the first time. Why is that?"

"Brains are funny things sometimes. Yours probably knew that if you stepped back and thought about everything as it was happening, you probably wouldn't have survived. I'm sure a therapist would be better equipped to answer that, though." I snorted at her response, aware that she was more tuned in to me than any therapist could ever hope, even more than Dr. Le Van. She brushed her fingers along the edge of the sheaf of papers, pushing it back into my hands. "It's yours." She turned to walk away, and I grabbed her hand, preventing her escape.

"You're going to leave today, aren't you?"

"Yes."

"Because this is how you still see me?" I held up the book in one hand, hoping she would tell me I was wrong, that she was leaving for some other reason.

She looked away, ashamed. "I…"

"You still think I am *this* child, the one who doesn't know what it is like to really feel? I am *not* her." The pitch of my voice rose an octave as I strained mightily to control the flood of sadness that threatened to wash me clean away from myself. The woman in front of me, with whom I had felt an unshakable kinship, the woman who wrote love songs in the empty space between the words in her book, thought me nothing more than a lost little girl? Was it pity that brought on her love? Obligation? Was it because I was the last tie to her father? Did she think it was the same for me, that my love rose from the embers of need that I had barely tended for all those years? I could feel myself shattering, pieces drifting off and floating in the still air of my living room, settling like dust on the surfaces I had come to know.

"I—"

I could not let her finish, knowing whatever she said would wound me deeper. "You want to believe that I don't know you, that we're strangers, but you tell my story better than I could tell it myself. You." I thrust my finger at her accusingly. "You tell me *I'm* not ready for the things I feel, even though I am. We're not so different, except I'm the one with the feelings now, and you're the child, closing herself off in an empty cave, refusing to see the lives being lived around her." I blinked furiously to stem the tears leaking down my cheeks.

Jessica threw her hands in the air. "You upended my entire world. I spent years without knowing the things you told me, and now it's shifting around inside me like a landmine, threatening to explode every time I take a step. I have no right to feel what I feel for you. For whatever reason, I am absolutely broken by you. After all you've been through, don't you want a normal life? An *easier* life?" She swiped angrily at her own tears, her voice soft and trembling as though she sought to control it.

"Who are you to tell me what a normal life is? I lived a normal life before I ever met you. This"—I swung an arm around me in a wide arc—"*this is not a normal life!* This is a lie that my head tells my heart every single day. This is a prison dressed up in pretty clothes and meaningless conversation. I will *never* be normal here, no matter how many things I learn or places I go."

"Welcome to real life," she countered quietly, tugging her hand from mine. "Do you think that every person you've met doesn't feel the same way? We are all damaged goods, Lily, no matter how we were raised."

I clenched my jaw against the truth she released into the air around us.

"Look, the reality is, you have been reborn into a world that will fall in love with you if you let it. You're going to meet lots of different people, ones who are much better for you than I am. After a while, after experiencing everything that will come to you, you'll look back and think 'gee, what a silly little crush I had,' and you'll shake your head in amusement as you move on. I can't be the reason you don't move on. I'd never forgive myself for shutting the door on all the possibilities awaiting you."

"So what I want doesn't matter?"

"Lily, I want to stay with you more than anything I've ever wanted. Nothing is ever as easy as it should be." She dropped a kiss on the top of my head and headed down the hallway to get ready to leave.

❖

The cottage grew smaller, tighter, suffocating me as I listened to the sound of her dressing. Before the bedroom door opened, I was gone, racing along the wet sand to escape the thundering of my breaking heart. Hours passed, the sun danced across the blue sky, the tide came and went. I thought of throwing myself into the ocean, swimming until my arms were limp as seaweed, giving myself to the dark water. It was no use, though; every time I stepped out farther, I would remember my mother. She had been so full of life in a way I could never quite grasp. Even when she was broken down by the death of my father, she'd found a way to show me how beautiful the world could be.

I sat in the wet sand, listening to the raspy calls of pelicans as they fished. The brutally honest fact was, this was no prison—the house, the clothes, the world at my fingertips— just squandered opportunities that I refused to allow myself to enjoy because I was too stubborn and too selfish. In the mountains, it was easy to nurture those flaws for the sake of survival, but here, they were open wounds that would not heal. Had I been born a pelican or a peacock, life would be simple. Eat, sleep, fly away at the first sign of danger. I had the misfortune of being born a human being, though, one who required more than just the barest necessities.

The sun began its slow descent, blurring the ocean and the horizon into similar shades of gray by the time I had gathered myself up. I dragged my exhausted body over the threshold and into the presence of Dawn, who sat in the lamplight with Jessica's book in her lap. I did not afford her a single glance as I clumped my way back to my bed and collapsed onto the thick mattress, overwhelmed with a lifetime of grief.

"Nothing I do will ever change any of this, will it?" Dawn's question was filled with resignation as she hovered at the side of the bed. "I was stupid to think I could have you back, have your mother back. If you had even once told me any of the things I just read about, maybe I could have figured it out before today." She let out a disgusted snort. "No, that's a lie. I probably would have continued to try to stuff you back down in my pocket in the hope that I could change you. I've made myself the fool this whole time, haven't I? My own grandmother used to say, 'the road to hell is paved with good intentions.' I never understood what she meant by that until right now." She sat and rested a hand on my back. I turned my head to face her as she spoke. "I hope you know I want nothing but good things for you, Lily. I might have tried to show it in a silly way, but it's true. When you were small, you were made of granite, hard and immovable. Like me, I suppose. Too closed off to feel what everyone else was feeling. It was stupid of me to assume nothing had changed and to try to change it myself so you could have a better life."

"I haven't changed at all."

"You are changing even at this very moment. You are all grown up. I can still see the granite in you, but there is so much more."

"I want to go home."

I was feeling raw and petulant, exposed by Jessica's writing, by her assurances that I was better off without her, by the realization that I would never be able to change her mind. It was as if I had finally started dying from the plane crash, like the memories themselves had created a new set of wounds that would bleed me dry. My entire story was about leaving, a cast of characters that paraded in through one door, across the stage, and out the other way. I thought the only way it would end was to be the one who left, to go back to the place I felt least affected. I knew Dr. Le Van would shake his head and tut-tut, telling me that running from my feelings was no way to live.

"But where is home?"

Her question threw me. Where was home? How could she not know where my home was? As I looked up at her, it slowly dawned on me that I had no idea how to answer her. It was home in Pennsylvania, where my mother's half-dead herb garden had lined the windowsill, and the neighborhood kids had ridden their bikes up and down the chalk graffitied sidewalks. It was home in the Ozarks, where the sun-dappled paths had stretched endlessly under the thick canopy of trees, and the birds had sung me awake every morning. It was home in Texas, where the warm sand had tickled between my toes, and the high water had left me gifts of opalescent shells and twisted driftwood artwork. These unimportant moments made a home inside me. They carved out little niches in my soul and set up altars as reminders of all the things I loved best.

My words tumbled out through heaving sobs. "I don't know."

Dawn grabbed my hand and held it to her breast, her normally stoic chin quivering slightly as she let out her breath. "I don't either, darling. I don't know what to do for you or how to help you find what you're looking for. It's clear to me that you aren't happy here. I would never sleep again if you went up north all by yourself, and it isn't safe for you to live the way you were in the woods. Plus, it's state-owned land."

"But the old man lived there."

"He did. His family probably owned that cabin for generations, but times have changed. There were no kin left to claim it, and the state finally just absorbed it into the rest of their holdings. There wasn't much left of it, either way, so they cleared the land."

"They tore it down?"

"Yes."

I could not fathom the woods without the overgrown field and ramshackle cabin. The first time I had seen it, I was terrified, dragged up onto the sagging porch by a stranger and his snarling dog to what seemed like my certain death. It had mirrored the old man in looks and sturdiness. Both were weathered and creaking, leaned a little to one side where they stood, and belonged exactly where they were. After his death, the heart went out of the place, and its flagging strength finally gave way. They were so interconnected, it seemed fitting that once one left this earth, the other had no choice but to follow.

"There is something else we need to talk about. What are we going to do about this?" She let go of my hand to tap the book she still held, drawing my attention to the stark white pages. "It's good. Jessica is an excellent writer. Doesn't she want to send it in to get published?"

"She didn't want it back." I had no idea what to make of Dawn's question. Why would anyone have any interest in an unremarkable girl snaring rabbits and picking berries in the wilds of Arkansas? What of my sad little existence could appeal to strangers?

"I have a friend who knows someone who could get this out in print. Would it bother you to have people read your story? It feels very...personal at spots, and there is a certain *undertone* that you may not want to broadcast to the world." The confusion no doubt brewing in my expression was enough to make her purse her lips. "You have spent a life sheltered from the emotions of others, Lily, and this book is written with the bravest of them all. It isn't a choice I would have made for you, but if this is the way I get to keep you, then I won't begrudge you my old-fashioned views. It is the twenty-first century, after all. I guess I should change with the times."

"What does that mean?"

"It means that the whole world will read this book and know exactly how the author feels about you. Will that bother you?"

"She left. Does it really matter? I'm just some dumb, backward kid, and she doesn't want to be around me."

"My God, sometimes you are so much like your mother, it makes me forget that you don't have the life experience to back it up." She shook her head in exasperation. "Lily, she is a completely different person from you, and you can't expect her to react to her feelings like you do. Give her some time."

"What if I never see her again?" I could feel the misery aching in my bone marrow, doing more damage than a snakebite ever could.

"Well, I can't promise you will, and I can't promise it won't hurt if you don't, but sometimes, that's how growing up goes. And about this"—Dawn held up the manuscript with both hands—"it matters more than you know. What she wrote, your story, it gives me hope. Hope that despite the harshness of reality, we can still be strong for those around us, hope that humanity exists even in the most remote places, hope that despite all the trauma, despite all the loss, we are capable of not only carrying on but of thriving. These are the things you represent to me. I forgot to keep living after I thought I had lost you and your mother. Everything I had loved in this world had disappeared that afternoon. Your grandfather, bless his soul, couldn't take the thought of living without his little girl, and he just...gave up. When he died, I kept soldiering on, but that wasn't any kind of life that I can remember. The day they called and told me about you, well, I thought it was some sick joke. When I saw you in that hospital, it was surreal. The only thing I could think about was taking you home and locking you in a safe little box where I would never have to think about losing you again. It killed me when you didn't recognize me. And when you wouldn't come with me...That was almost worse than losing you in the first place. I never thought I would be a stranger to the only family I had left in the world."

She took a moment to collect herself before she continued, picking at a loose thread on the comforter. "I can't begin to understand what you went through out there or even what you are going through right now, but I do know that no matter what, I will be here. We will figure out how to be friends, how to be a family. Don't make the same mistakes I did, shriveling up till I was nothing but an empty vessel waiting for the good Lord to come and take me way. You're a blank slate, *dammit*, with decades of joy and heartache and discovery waiting to be had." She sat me up in the bed, brushing the tangles from my face, and gave me a firm shake. "You are the best of all of us, and there isn't a thing you can do to change it. We need to put our heads together and fix this."

CHAPTER THIRTEEN

Eighteen months later

The truth was, time did *not* heal all wounds. Time made the aching a little less and the sadness a little easier to stomach, but the wound remained. It allowed me to gingerly adapt to the pain, to learn how to put it in a box on a high shelf in the farthest reaches of my mind and to pretend I'd forgotten it, though the lid gathered no dust from how often it was taken down and peered into. Time created a perfect little glass sculpture of the thing I longed for, devoid of any visible flaws, and sat it where the light just barely reached, just barely glinted off the curves, so I always had it dancing in my peripheral vision.

Time provided the winding path for me to travel, and I chose to put one foot in front of the other. It was difficult at first, shuffling steps from the cottage to the house, from the patio to the surf, from the dawn to the dusk, but I realized giving up would be even harder. I had survived this long, and heartbreak would not be the sword that ended me. It helped to have family and friends who gave me their all, no matter how miserably and intolerably I behaved. Honestly, without Charlie and Dawn, it would have been an impossible task.

Dawn pushed me harder than I thought was possible, seeing to it that I finished my GED and got accepted into a college program for Environmental Science and Sustainability. I ended my first semester with honors that she gleefully bragged about to the rest of the country club set. I loved every minute of school. It was astounding how much information existed about the natural world and humbling to learn how I, one single person, could make a difference.

Charlie, my own personal sounding board, let me work through all the emotions I had spent my life squashing down. He sat with me through tears and laughter, through bitter and sweet, proving to me that soulmates came in all forms. When he met the love of his life, Andrea, at a Rangers game, she slid right into our twosome like we had been waiting for her the whole time. She was soft and pretty, like an old-timey actress, and she looked at him with big, adoring eyes. She loved nature almost as much as I did, so the three of us spent a lot of time hiking, camping, and exploring whenever classes allowed. I couldn't explain the warmth and joy I felt watching them smile their goofy smiles at each other.

Hugo, the long-suffering gardener who'd put up with all the craziness we could throw at him, finally relented and taught me how to drive his battered, rattletrap pickup truck. After months of lessons, I had a shiny new driver's license to put in my wallet. I fell in love with his old death trap, and despite the utter disgust on Dawn's face, she convinced him to give me the truck in exchange for a newer model. He pretended to be devastated at the loss of his favorite ride, but I would often catch him admiring the pristine red paint on his new F-350 with a dreamy look in his eye.

The biggest change, though, was where I hung my hat. On three clear acres of heaven in the Ozarks, Dawn helped me build a little cabin. It nestled in the backwoods country, far enough from civilization that I could feel the mountains in my bones but close enough that it still had high-speed internet and an endless supply of hot water. A mailbox and a broad hawthorn tree, carved with a circle and five dots, marked the beginning of the driveway.

I paid my own way as I could, working for the Arkansas Game and Fish Commission, keeping the mountain safe for wildlife and tourists. Sometimes, I would lead hikers on guided tours, teaching them the basics of being environmentally responsible. I also had the pleasure of sniffing out the occasional poacher and sending them straight into the arms of local law enforcement. They were small victories, nothing that would change the fate of the world, but it healed little bits of the past for me.

Dawn had spent two months supervising the cabin building process, micromanaging the workers, and being a general nuisance, yet I could not complain since she was footing the bill, and it gave me the freedom to be myself once more. Convinced she needed to be near me, she purchased land and had a ridiculously large house built on the outskirts of the nearest town. She stayed there more than her home in Texas, grousing about the locals and their "lack of couth" as she sat on her front porch enjoying the views of Spanish moss–covered cypress trees and wildflower fields. One thing she made me promise was that I would not hide away from her and the rest of the world. We had an agreement that when she was back in Texas, I would visit her twice a month, and when she was staying at the house close by, I would meet her three times a week for dinner…formal, of course.

The cabin was larger than I had originally wanted, but Dawn had insisted on space for guests as she planned to visit often despite its remote location and less-than-optimal access. Though miles and miles from the waterfall of my youth, the crash site, and the old man's place, it was home nonetheless. It was surrounded by the mountains that had become such an integral part of me through the years.

As much as I hated to admit it, civilized living had grown on me, and I was spoiled for technology, loving the access to the unlimited information the internet provided. My days were filled with living: work, classes, walking in the woods with my dogs, tending the chickens and other various critters I had acquired, sitting in front of a roaring fire and reading long into the night.

The neighbors, though few and far between, looked after one another fiercely, pulling me into their tight circle of friends as though I had always been there. I belonged in a way I had never experienced, not in my childhood, not in my cave, not in Texas. Mountain people, the heart of the Ozarks, embraced me and invited me into their close-knit community, filling me with a sense of family. I didn't know whether they'd read my story or had heard it by word of mouth or if their kindness was just a genuine reflection of the innate goodness of a people not burdened by society's demanding pace. No one questioned my right to be among them. They shared themselves, their skills, and their friendship completely.

Despite all this, there was still a hidden ache inside, buried beneath the stacks of happiness, the wound that time could not heal. I shamelessly googled Jessica Velasquez, watching her life play out on the small monitor in my living room. I read every article she had written, looked at every picture, listened to every little sound bite, but it was never enough. I could still feel the burn of her fingertips against mine as though she was a phantom limb.

Her book crept up the best sellers list, and we were both pushed further into the public eye. When the first reviews came out, Dawn swooped in through the front door of my sanctuary, not bothering to knock, beaming as she waved a stack of papers under my nose.

"And you thought no one would be interested!" She did a little spin and dip, dancing around the couch in an unusual display of joy. "Your Jessica is making quite a name for the two of you."

I snatched up the papers, scanning them with growing surprise. It was disconcerting to have the whole world read the intimate details of my life, startling that anyone would want to, and overwhelming to read beautiful reviews by strangers. I couldn't help but feel a sense of pride for Jessica's success. She deserved it.

After that, I was occasionally accosted by a reporter at the little grocery store or the gas station. The proprietors, my protective mountain people, ran them off, cackling with delight. Rarely, I would consent to a short interview or picture, and it seemed Jessica was of the same mind. Her private life remained a mystery to me, other than the snippets and photos I gleaned from the internet. I would stare at each picture and hope she was happy wherever she was, that she had come to grips with whatever monsters she was fighting.

❖

The rain had been falling steadily all morning, thick sheets cascading over the windshield of my truck as I left the grocery store. The stony driveway leading to the cabin was nearly impassable in the best of conditions, but the wet spring weather had left it slickened to treacherous proportions. The four-wheel drive managed it, the pickup fishtailing here and there in the deeper ruts. Red clay speckled its green paint, almost obscuring the scratches and dents underneath. I rounded the last switchback to the clearing, and the rain petered out, turning from a heavy downpour to a feathery mist while steam rose from the heat of decaying leaves on the ground. The engine rumbled low past the woodshed and chicken house, past the hidden trailheads, echoing softly in the stillness of the mountains. As the sound of the motor cut out, the wilderness relaxed into a symphony of birds and insects strumming the music of renewal and rebirth. This was my home.

My hiking boots crunched across the gravel at the front of the cabin, alerting the welcoming committee of my presence. I could hear them braying mournfully behind the oak door, scratching and whining as I climbed the few steps onto the porch toting an armload of grocery bags. I struggled with the key, dropping it twice in an effort not to pitch the items out of their bags. When I opened the front door and tossed my keys on the entryway table, I was nearly smothered under the greeting of Honey and Truffle, red and white coonhounds that had been a gift from Charlie. They were still young, not quite a year, full of energy and overflowing with love. They *almost* filled the Biscuit-sized hole that still resided in my heart. They knocked the bags out of my hands, spilling them along the glossy wooden floor and into the main room of the cabin. I could not bear to scold them for their enthusiasm as I gathered up the goods to take to the kitchen, dogs leaping and prancing around me joyously.

I was prepping for a hiking trip with Charlie and Andrea that would take up the whole weekend. I had been exploring new areas and had found a hot spring off the beaten path that I couldn't wait to share with my friends. The area was secluded and beautiful, almost as remote as the little pool I had grown up around. It was my turn to get the goodies together that we would need for two nights away. Honestly, I could have done without all the packaged food, knowing that there was enough to forage so I wouldn't be hungry, but my friends had insisted on s'mores and mountain pies.

I brought most of the gear outside to fill my pack in the sunshine that blazed on the wet grass, watching Honey and Truffle chase one another through the perimeter of trees, stirring up rabbits and squirrels as they tore through the underbrush, rolling and wrestling. They were as excited as I was to spend a few nights in the wild. Still in training, they needed to be leashed when we left the property and spent nights zipped up in my tent so their puppy chaos was contained while I slept. Honey was a little more laid-back, more inclined to stay at my heels than Truffle, who found more trouble than I ever imagined possible. I had become an expert at plucking out porcupine quills, dressing scrapes and scratches, and wrapping sore paws when the exuberant dog ignored common sense and barreled into danger with a wagging tail. She kept me on my toes.

I walked back in the cabin for a few more items, checking off my to-do list absentmindedly. I still needed to check the tent, reorganize the first aid kit, and fold up a few extra pieces of clothing for my pack. I wanted to make sure I had my binoculars and bird book, too. The bray of my overzealous pups brought me back to reality, and I trotted back outside to see what was causing the commotion.

Sun glinted off the top of a car that was covered to the windows in a thick cake of mud as it drew to a stop beside my truck. How it had ever made the treacherous drive to the cabin was baffling. I stood stock still as a young woman climbed out, shading her eyes with her hand as she faced me from fifty paces away. Jessica.

She made it two steps before being overcome by canines and squatted in the center of the wriggling, wagging dogs, laughing at their yips for attention. I stayed frozen on the porch, fearful that if I moved, the mirage would dissipate.

"It's beautiful up here," she called from the stony driveway. "Exactly how I pictured it."

"It really is," I managed to squeeze out through my constricted throat.

"How have you been?"

I furrowed my brow a bit, knowing there wasn't a safe answer to be found. I could tell her the truth and let her know how much I'd missed her or lie and tell her I had been just peachy on my own. Neither answer felt like a good idea. Instead, I froze and waited for her to say something else.

She stood and brushed at the muddy paw prints smeared across her blue jeans. Holding my breath as she walked toward me, I watched a familiar smile pull at the corners of her mouth. She mounted the steps, stopping a few feet from me as we regarded one another in silence. All the photographs I had gawked at on the internet did not do justice to her. She had matured in a way I could not quite place, wearing confidence like a tailored jacket across her broad shoulders. When she slipped the sunglasses off, her dark eyes had a new cast, intense and magnetic, finally seeming comfortable in her own skin. I drank in the slight smell of her perfume, feeling layers of dust shed from the shelves of my heart, unearthing memories I had abandoned in my grief.

"Been a while, huh?"

"It has." Despite every ache she had caused me, I was more in love with her now than I had ever been. I would have forgiven her anything just to snatch a few moments of her time. I could learn to be happy with that.

"Going somewhere?" She pointed at the pack I had dropped at my feet.

"Camping with friends."

"Think you might have room for one more?"

I had no idea how to respond.

She squeezed her eyes shut for a moment and took a deep breath. "You have every right to be pissed at me. I'm a complete boob. It took me about five minutes to realize I had made a terrible mistake when I left, but I was too ashamed of myself to come back, and I was too scared that I had ruined everything. It turns out, I have no freaking clue how to let myself be happy. I thought that if I didn't know how to make myself happy, there's no way I could make someone else happy. I didn't want to give it a chance because I knew I'd screw it up, and it would hurt even worse. If you'll let me, I'd like to start over. I understand if you don't want to. I wouldn't be inclined to give me another chance, either."

Before I could answer, the dogs went wild again, racing to meet the Jeep coming up the driveway. Andrea and Charlie hopped out and walked up to the porch holding hands.

"S'up?" Charlie drawled, tilting his chin at Jessica and winking.

"S'up?" She smiled and raised her eyebrows at Andrea.

"This is my other half, Andrea. This is Jessica."

"*The* Jessica? Damn. I wish I would have known. I would've brought my book to be signed." She looked at me and leaned close to whisper loudly in my ear. "She's a fox, girl. I can see why you're so hung up on her. If I wasn't with the old ball and chain, here, I'd be tempted to hop the fence." She burst out laughing as I blushed furiously.

"Behave yourself, woman." Charlie growled, pulling her into his arms. He turned to Jessica and shrugged. "Can't take this one anywhere without her causing trouble. It's her best quality."

"Seems like you met your match."

"Peas in a pod, we are. Glad you could make it today."

Once again, my best friend had conspired against me, and I wanted to hate him for it. One day, I would find a way to pay him back for all the times he'd cooked up schemes behind my back.

"I was just asking Lily if she minded me tagging along."

"Looks like you guys already planned for it, so I don't get a say," I grumbled, trying to hide the panic I was feeling. A weekend in the woods was one thing, but having to spend it with the person who'd made a career out of devastating me sounded like torture.

Jessica's face fell. "If you don't want—"

"So it's all settled, then," Charlie interrupted, smirking. "Finish packing up, and let's hit the trail, ladies." Andrea shook her head and snickered, making me think that she was all too aware of my best friend's treasonous behavior.

"You bring a bag?" I asked.

My question seemed to throw Jessica. She stared at me for a long moment, stroking the soft ear of Honey, who leaned against her leg, then nodded. I looked at her hiking boots and sighed. I finished slipping items into my pack, then hefted it onto my back while she rifled around in the back of her car.

"Ready when you are," she said softly, walking back to where the three of us had collected.

I pointed toward the far end of the property where a tiny opening in the thick underbrush marked the beginning of the trail. "It's tight at first but opens up farther in."

It was still chilly under the trees, the ground slick from the morning rain and steaming where the sun hit. Nobody really spoke for the first half hour as we hiked on the trail that was only wide enough for one person. Once it widened, Andrea stepped up beside me, asking questions about where we were going. I answered half-heartedly, focusing my senses on Jessica, who walked a few feet behind me chatting with Charlie. I could feel the soft rumble of her voice across my skin leaving tingling trails up and down my arms.

After a while, Andrea punched me in the arm and huffed. "You could at least pretend to listen to me, Lil. I might as well be talking to the dogs."

"Sorry," I mumbled, turning my head slightly to see behind me. They were probably twenty feet back, laughing at something I hadn't heard.

Andrea grabbed the leashes from my hands and rolled her eyes. "How about you quit acting like a wuss and go talk to her already? I'm not spending the next two days watching this. It's excruciating." She waved for Charlie to follow and walked off down the path, leaving me to face Jessica alone.

She fell in step beside me, and when I locked eyes with her, my brain turned to jelly. All I could think about was the feel of her lips, wet and velvety against my own. I didn't realize that we had stopped walking until she reached out and brushed my hair behind my ear.

"I really have missed you, Lily," she said, her voice low and rough. "You were right, you know. No one knows how things are going to pan out. No one can predict the future."

"You seemed to think you could."

"Yeah. I guess I did. Turns out, I was wrong. I chose to be miserable and alone because I thought I would end up miserable and alone. It took a lot of self-reflection to realize how utterly stupid that was." She smiled, but it looked more like a grimace. "Well, that and a stern talking-to by Mr. Persuasive over there."

We both looked toward Charlie, who turned his head away, apparently pretending he hadn't been watching us the whole time. His smirk gave him away.

"Did you ever send him those flowers?"

"Wha...*Oh*." She snorted with laughter. "I did, actually. Did you know he's allergic to daffodils?"

"Mmm-hmm. He's allergic to *everything*. We went berry picking last year, and he left the farm looking like we should have put him in the basket with the rest of the strawberries. He had hives for a week."

"Please tell me you got pictures of it."

"Ask Andrea. She took about a hundred and posted them online. I'm sure she'd be happy to embarrass him some more and show them off to you."

"Noted."

"What did he say to convince you to show up?"

"He told me exactly what kind of fool I was, no-holds-barred. He also told me I didn't deserve someone like you, and if I was going to keep up this dumb charade, he would pay someone to have me tossed from the top of the highest tower. Then he said you guys were going camping, and if I was going to fix this, I better bring my sexiest long underwear and a well-thought-out apology."

"And did you?"

"Well, I wouldn't necessarily say it's the *sexiest* long underwear, but it does the job. As for the apology..." She dropped to her knees so quickly, I thought she had fallen. "I *am* sorry. Sorry I hurt you and sorry I let my insecurities get in the way of my heart. I know nothing I say will undo the past, and I know that I'm far enough from perfect that I'll probably screw up pretty often, but I can't spend another day without you. I've never felt like this before. It's terrifying. It feels like I'm stepping off a ledge into the unknown. Every single second of our lives, every decision, every action and reaction has led us both to this exact moment. Call it destiny, fate, kismet, whatever word you want to use, I know this is the place I belong. I know that I will never be the same after knowing you, and even if you send me on my way, I'll be content to keep this flame burning for the rest of my life. I love you, Lily Andrews. I'll always love you. Will you give me one last chance to prove it?"

As she knelt in front of me, I could see the little girl in the picture from Jack's wallet, the girl who had sat across the campfire from me, the girl who had stared at my nakedness on the dunes, and the girl who had bared her true feelings in the lines of a book. They were all tiny creeks feeding the river of her, strong and constant, the current swift against my rocky shores. There was tremendous beauty in her honesty, and it peeled away the chaos of our entanglement until there was nothing but the living roots, the tendrils that connected us like mushrooms and mountains and stardust.

I had spent a lifetime towing the weight of my feelings behind me like a broken-down wagon, struggling against wheels that would not turn. When I had finally unpacked it, taking out each individual feeling and examining it for what it was, I'd found that I was not an awkward little girl who chose the forest, but a full-grown woman, capable of all sorts of incredible things. The most incredible of them all was happiness.

I saw it in the dark eyes that gazed up at me, in the tentative smile, in the broad shoulders and freckles and long braid. There was nothing to forgive her for. Nothing she had done could overshadow the happiness that warmed me when I looked at her. She made me feel like the only wildflower in the vastness of the Ozarks, ready to bloom at her touch.

I knelt amid the wet leaves and pine needles, reaching across the space that separated us. When the tips of my fingers touched hers, I could feel her trembling, a shake that seemed all too familiar.

"Is…is that a yes?" Her expression was a mixture of hope and fear.

I laced my fingers with hers, squeezing softly. "It was always a yes."

Charlie and Andrea let out a whoop, startling the dogs into a barking frenzy and scaring every bird on the mountainside. "It's about damn time," Charlie yelled, clapping.

Epilogue

That homey little cabin in the woods hosted three more generations under our watchful eyes. I saw my children and grandchildren and great-grandchildren play on the fallen trees out back. I rocked them in the swing on the porch and tended their scratches at the kitchen table. I saw them grow to be doctors and scientists and ecologists and journalists. And I did it with the woman who made me whole.

I spent decades with the love of my life beside the stone fireplace in the living room. I watched her brush her teeth every morning, watched her tapping away at the keys of her laptop in the evenings, watched her grow even more beautiful as time passed. Our house was filled with love, with photographs, with memories and joy. A thousand little altars in my heart paid homage to the life I'd led, to the homes I had known and the people I had loved.

When, one day, Jessica and I broke the bonds of life and truly became part of this mountain together, we reached out our roots far and wide, grew without borders, without clocks, without fear and sadness. Our love kept us growing until we stretched across the cosmos, until we found the fraying ends of eternity, and that, too, we surpassed.

About the Author

A native Pennsylvanian and a HACC, EGCC, and WGU alumna, Cathleen "Cat" Collins has been fascinated with words for as long as she can remember. She started out writing poetry and short stories, but somehow, enough characters wiggled their way into her thoughts that she had to put them on paper. Thanks to a vast network of friends (both in person and in the magical land of the internet) cheering her on, she has started more projects than she could ever possibly finish. All her work is centered around the L in LGBTQ+ and varies from paranormal/fantasy to plain old romance to feral children (and, let's be honest, who doesn't love feral children?).

After a complete 180-degree career change from the night shift world of caring for developmentally disabled adults to the 9–5 daylight world of personal income tax, Cat has learned to be even more thankful for every day and every person she meets. She is currently working toward a bachelor's degree in elementary and special education, and who knows where that may lead?

Cat spends her free time lounging about the farmette she shares with her partner of two decades, Lori, and their menagerie of horses, cats, dogs, and feathered friends. She enjoys starting construction projects she will never truly complete, growing a jungle of vegetables, and pretending she doesn't like to bake.

You can email Cat, find her perusing all the crazy cat groups on Facebook, or follow all her chaos and shenanigans on Instagram. Since technology is the bane of her simple existence, she will most likely never tweet, hashtag, or TikTok her way into internet infamy without encouragement from a high voltage cattle prod or a carrot stick baited with peanut butter cups.

Books Available From Bold Strokes Books

Crush by Ana Hartnett Reichardt. Josie Sanchez worked for years for the opportunity to create her own wine label, and nothing will stand in her way. Not even Mac, the owner's annoyingly beautiful niece Josie's forced to hire as her harvest intern. (978-1-63679-330-6)

Decadence by Ronica Black, Renee Roman & Piper Jordan. You are cordially invited to Decadence, Las Vegas's most talked about invitation-only Masquerade Ball. Come for the entertainment and stay for the erotic indulgence. We guarantee it'll be a party that lives up to its name. (978-1-63679-361-0)

Gimmicks and Glamour by Lauren Melissa Ellzey. Ashly has learned to hide her Sight, but as she speeds toward high school graduation she must protect the classmates she claims to hate from an evil that no one else sees. (978-1-63679-401-3)

Heart of Stone by Sam Ledel. Princess Keeva Glantor meets Maeve, a gorgon forced to live alone thanks to a decades-old lie, and together the two women battle forces they formerly thought to be good in the hopes of leading lives they can finally call their own. (978-1-63679-407-5)

Peaches and Cream by Georgia Beers. Adley Purcell is living her dreams owning Get the Scoop ice cream shop until national dessert chain Sweet Heaven opens less than two blocks away and Adley has to compete with the far too heavenly Sabrina James. (978-1-63679-412-9)

The Only Fish in the Sea by Angie Williams. Will love overcome years of bitter rivalry for the daughters of two crab fishing families in this queer modern-day spin on Romeo and Juliet? (978-1-63679-444-0)

Wildflower by Cathleen Collins. When a plane crash leaves eleven-year-old Lily Andrews stranded in the vast wilderness of Arkansas, will she be able to overcome the odds and make it back to civilization and the one person who holds the key to her future? (978-1-63679-621-5)

Witch Finder by Sheri Lewis Wohl. Tasmin, the Keeper of the Book of Darkness, is in terrible danger, and as a Witch Finder, Morrigan must protect her and the secrets she guards even if it costs Morrigan her life. (978-1-63679-335-1)

Digging for Heaven by Jenna Jarvis. Litz lives for dragons. Kella lives to kill them. The last thing they expect is to find each other attractive. (978-1-63679-453-2)

Forever's Promise by Missouri Vaun. Wesley Holden migrated west disguised as a man for the hope of a better life and with no designs to take a wife, but Charlotte Rose has other ideas. (978-1-63679-221-7)

Here For You by D. Jackson Leigh. A horse trainer must make a difficult business decision that could save her father's ranch from foreclosure but destroy her chance to win the heart of a feisty barrel racer vying for a spot in the National Rodeo Finals. (978-1-63679-299-6)

I Do, I Don't by Joy Argento. Creator of the romance algorithm, Nicole Hart doesn't expect to be starring in her own reality TV dating show, and falling for the show's executive producer Annie Jackson could ruin everything. (978-1-63679-420-4)

It's All in the Details by Dena Blake. Makeup artist Lane Donnelly and wedding planner Helen Trent can't stand each other, but they must set aside their differences to ensure Darcy gets the wedding of her dreams, and make a few of their own dreams come true. (978-1-63679-430-3)

Marigold by Melissa Brayden. Marigold Lavender vows to take down Alexis Wakefield, the harsh food critic who blasts her younger sister's restaurant. If only she wasn't as sexy as she is mean. (978-1-63679-436-5)

A Second Chance at Life by Genevieve McCluer. Vampires Dinah and Rachel reconnect, but a string of vampire killings begin and evidence seems to be pointing at Dinah. They must prove her innocence while finding out if the two of them are still compatible after all these years. (978-1-63679-459-4)

The Town That Built Us by Jesse J. Thoma. When her father dies, Grace Cook returns to her hometown and tries to avoid Bonnie Whitlock, the woman who pulverized her heart, only to discover her father's estate has been left to them jointly. (978-1-63679-439-6)